BIG LONESOME

JIM RULAND

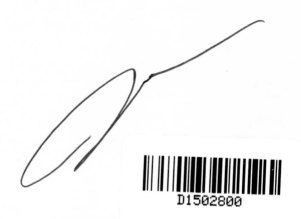

D1502800

GORSKY PRESS
LOS ANGELES • CALIFORNIA
2005

Published by
Gorsky Press
P.O. Box 42024
Los Angeles, CA 90042

ISBN 0-9753964-3-9

cover art by Dave Guthrie
author photo by Cynthia Pallin

Slightly different versions of these stories previously appeared in the
following publications: "Night Soil Man" in *Quarterly West* and *The
God Particle*; "The Previous Adventures of Popeye the Sailor" in *Black
Warrior Review*; "Kessler Has No Lucky Pants" in *The Barcelona
Review*; "A Terrible Thing in a Place Like This" in *Fictionline* and
Punch & Pie; "Pronto's Persistence" in *Sweet Fancy Moses*; "Dick
Tracy on the Moon" in *The American Journal of Print*; and "The
Hitman's Handbook" in *Blue Murder*.

for Annie

BIG LONESOME

JIM RULAND

NIGHT SOIL MAN

The Bellevue Pleasure Gardens was a large park at the end of the tramline that featured tidy gardens, a teahouse, and views of the city. The Belfast Corporation added the zoological specimens later. Apes and elephants. Bears and birds. A few days after his seventeenth birthday, the corporation relieved Simon Boone of his duties on the tramline and transferred him to the zoo to clean the cages. The work suits him, but now his mates call him Simon the Night Soil Man, Shite Shovelin' Boone. Simon pretends he can't hear them, but it bothers him more than he lets on. Sometimes it makes him mad enough to want to quit, but only sometimes.

Simon makes his way down Great Victoria Street to The Bridge, a pub near the city centre in Shaftsbury Square. The gentlemen expecting him this afternoon— Alex Johnson and Dick Stepford—are already at the bar, making quick work of their healers, as nervous as a couple of birds.

"Hello, Simon. How's the boxing coming along?"

"Fine. Thanks for asking."

"Have one with us?" Alex asks.

"I'll have a milk."

"Milk?" Dick makes no effort to hide his disgust.

"Aye. It's grand for the bones." Simon rolls up his shirtsleeve and gives the arm a flex.

"That's yer muscles, you eejit," Dick says. "Yer bones are all in yer head."

"Right then. Make it a pint."

That gets them all laughing, but it dries up quick. They didn't come here for laughs. The bartender gets the Guinness going. Alex pays.

Alex is the curator; Dick is the zookeeper. Alex is an old footballer with drooping mustaches and hair that curls around his ears. Middle age has been kind to him and he still looks like he could do some damage on the pitch. Dick looks ten years Alex's senior, though the two are nearly identical in age. He's soft-spoken, but direct, just the sort of man you'd expect would be good with animals. His features betray the long hours he spends outside.

Last week Alex called Simon into his office and asked him if he'd be up for a special, after-hours assignment. Simon said he would. The extra few quid would go a long way.

No one speaks until Simon is squared up with a pint. He drains half the glass with his first swallow. By the look of things, he has some catching up to do.

"Dirty bit of business," Dick mutters.

"It is indeed," Alex replies.

"I don't fancy it. Not in the least."

"None of us do, Dick. But it's got to be done, and we're the fellows for it."

"Bloody war," Dick says.

He's in a black mood, blacker than usual. Alex keeps shooting Simon looks as if to apologize for Dick's poor humor. He needn't bother. Simon's a volunteer. He'll do as he's told.

"Another, gents?" the bartender asks.

"Aye," they say as one.

Simon pays. The men mumble their thanks and retreat to their thoughts. Dick keeps looking at his watch. At five o'clock Alex orders whiskeys.

"Courage," he says by way of a toast.

They make music with the glasses and take their medicine.

"Come. I'll show you the works."

Alex has one of the Corporation's panel trucks parked out back. He opens the passenger door and removes a rifle case from under the seat. He opens it up and shows them the well-oiled weapon.

".303?" Dick asks.

"Aye. There's two more just like it under the seat. Think that'll do the job?"

Dick goes quiet, calculating the equations.

"What about you?" Alex says to Simon. "If you want out, now's the time to say so."

"I'm ready. Ready for anything."

The thing is none of them want to shoot the animals.

The Germans bombed the city a week ago. The blitz caught them unawares, killed eleven people. A deputation

11

of citizens from the Antrim Road petitioned the Belfast Corporation to have the specimens removed or eliminated. That's what they called them: specimens. An air raid, the committee argued, was one thing, dangerous animals unleashed on the streets of Belfast quite another. On Thursday the Corporation announced its decision: destroy the animals.

Alex was furious. He raged all day, slamming doors and kicking over trash bins. Dick went off to tend the animals and didn't come back to the office until well past closing. They agreed to carry out the orders, but come Friday no one was up for the task.

"Let's enjoy our weekend in peace," Alex had said.

"That go for the Germans as well?" Simon asked.

"Feck the Germans," Dick spat.

Alex has a bottle in the truck. By the time they get to the zoo they are properly polluted. They leave the truck near the gates and stagger up the escarpment with the rifles slung clumsily over their shoulders. They look like gravediggers on a lark.

They start at the paddock where Billie the Asian elephant is kept. Billie is the zoo's main attraction. The Belfast Corporation bought her from a traveling circus after she slipped her chains in Bombay. There are no chains at the Bellevue Pleasure Garden; Billie is free to roam her paddock as she pleases. She's a natural talent. When the mood strikes her, she gets up on her hind legs and balances on one massive foot, trumpeting proudly. Sometimes Simon brings her droppings home for the garden and Ma's tomatoes are the pride of the Shankill.

Dick loves Billie. He says he can read her just by

looking at her eyes. One look at Dick tells them he isn't ready for this, so they move on to the tiger cages. Both the Bengal tigers, Jasmine and Fulaka, are out by the pool.

"Who wants to go first?" Alex asks.

No one volunteers. Simon decided back at The Bridge to keep his gob shut. Once they put down the animals he'll be out of a job, but if they put a good word in for him there's a chance he can stay on with the Corporation without having to go back to the trams.

"Maybe we should all fire at once," Dick says.

"Aye," Simon agrees. "Like a firing squad."

Alex nods at the soundness of the plan.

They unpack their rifles, load the weapons, throw the bolts home. Alex tests his sling. Dick holds the rifle like he's considering pitching it into the pool. They smoke fags while they decide which cat to shoot first. Jasmine is the more ornery of the two. Fulaka is a layabout who on some days can scarcely be bothered to feed himself. Jasmine's the one. Sorry Jasmine.

They aim and fire. The reports echo through the zoo. Over in the aviary, the birds make an awful row, rising up into the caged air with nowhere to go. Jasmine twitches her tail. Fulaka doesn't wake up, the bastard.

"I wasn't even close," Alex confesses. His face is red from drink, anger, and embarrassment.

"I didn't see where mine went," says Dick. "Did you?"

Simon shakes his head. His shot went high, but he keeps it to himself.

"Let's have another go," Alex says.

Simon's aim is off and his shot goes high again, higher than before. Alex looks suspiciously at his rifle. Dick is disgusted with himself, the whole sad affair. He sets his rifle down and sits on the kerb.

"I can't do this," he says. "I can't even feckin' see straight. What if we only wound the poor buggers? The people of Antrim Road with their bleedin' deputations and committees can feck off as far I'm concerned."

Alex makes a study of the sky, squinting up at the places where the stars will soon peek through.

"It's getting dark," he says. "Maybe we should wait until morning."

Dick and Simon agree without hesitation. They put the rifles back in their cases. It feels as if a terrible burden has been lifted, a heavy yoke cast off. Jasmine yawns, ignorant of her fate.

Simon, his younger brother Brian, and their Ma have been on their own for over a year now. They used to be four, but Da died a year ago March. He was a sailor, a seaman in the merchant fleet out of Liverpool. He served as a quartermaster on the *Gregory Dunston*, a tanker carrying rubber from Bermuda. The Germans hit her amidships with a torpedo that broke her in half. There were no survivors, but sometimes Simon wonders. Da had a survival belt equipped with matches, fishhooks, a compass, and a flask of rum to keep his spirits up. He knew the risks, he wrote in his letters. He was ready for anything.

Sometimes Simon thinks about that when he's in the ring. He can be ready for only a few things at a time: a quick jab with the left leads to a right, a dip in the shoulder means a hard one's coming low. Right when he thinks he's got his man beat is when he usually finds himself on his backside marveling at the brightness of the lights, the darkness of just about everything else.

Da was mad for maps and charts. He knew his business. He wouldn't have needed much to get himself out of a tight spot. What if he'd found a spar, a hatch cover to cling to? What if he made it off the ship alive?

Ma doesn't care much for Simon's what-ifs. She took the news hard, went into a bit of shock. She stopped eating and her teeth fell out. Brian buried himself in his books. One of Da's old shipmates fixed Simon up with a job with the Belfast Corporation, cleaning tram stations. Now he's the man of the family, such as he is, such as they are.

When Simon went to work hauling shite at Bellevue, Ma told him Da used to take her up there when they were courting. Simon doesn't believe it. The past, to hear Ma tell it, was a rosy place full of dances and tea parties. Da hadn't been around much, but Simon wants to remember him the way he was: stern, blunt, sparse with the kind word, but fair. He never hit them out of turn and he always had gifts for them when he came back from sea.

After a few months on the job Simon started dreaming about Jasmine. It always started the same way: Simon was closing up for the night, coming down the cinder path toward the main gate with his shovel—and there she was. She always saw him before he saw her. He never knew if he should run or stand his ground, and the indecision paralyzed him. Jasmine chased him down dense jungles and dark lanes until there was nowhere else to go—the proverbial end of the line. Then Brian jolted him awake with a sharp kick.

"Quiet! You'll wake Da!"

But Da was dead. He couldn't hear Simon no matter how loud he cried.

Simon wakes with a start, bright lights booming all around. Bloody hell, he thinks, I missed the job.

They'd been sitting on an old horse blanket in the Pleasure Gardens proper, nipping at a bottle of Powers. They must have dozed off for a good bit because now the city is lit up brighter than Christmas. Giant flares float down on parachutes, illuminating the bellies of the German Junkers emptying their payloads as they streak across the sky.

Dick is out cold on the blanket. Simon gives him a shove as another wave of planes comes screaming over the Black Mountains. Dick sits up. They scramble up the slope, their hangovers forgotten.

The next wave of Junkers drop bombs that detonate with such force they send massive geysers of earth and stone twenty meters into the air. Alex leads them to a concrete utility shed where the tractors are stored and they take cover under the stairs. Down in the city, an air raid siren warbles like a great bird of mourning.

"Shite," Dick murmurs over and over again.

The bombing lasts all night. The raiders come out of the north, down the Antrim Road and turn around at the lough to give it another go with their bombs and parachute mines. The Whitewell and Crumlin Roads are hit hardest. The shipyards at Harland & Wolf take a beating, as do Mackies and the Sirocco ventilator works. A pall of smoke from the many fires hangs over the city, making it difficult

16

to see where the damage has been done.

It's a hundred times worse than the raid last week, but no bombs fall on the zoo. They consider taking aim at the planes with their .303s, but they are hopelessly out of range. The only resistance comes from *HMS Furious* sitting in for repairs. The belching of her guns can be heard in the distance. All they can do is curse.

Throughout the night the lesser game bellow in their cages. Billie trumpets without respite. The desperation in it is a torment to poor Dick.

At five o'clock in the morning the all-clear siren sounds. The ghost of the sun limns the edge of the lough and is refracted through the smoke of a hundred fires.

They gather at the tiger cage. Jasmine has taken cover in a niche between boulders. She always was a right smart girl. Fulaka suns himself by the pool. Dick pops off two rounds before Alex and Simon are settled. The crack of the rifle startles them.

Jasmine and Fulaka lie perfectly still. Dick unlocks the cage and goes inside. He checks on Jasmine first, then Fulaka.

"That do it then?" Alex calls out.

"Aye," Dick answers.

He exits the cage and locks it up again before starting up the path toward the savanna.

"I'm off to do some big game hunting," he says. He tries to make a joke of it, but there are tears in his eyes and something in his voice neither one of them has heard before. Simon watches a red peninsula of Fulaka's blood ooze toward the tiger pool and he wonders if he's going to have to clean it when the killing's done.

"Dick has the right idea," Alex says.

"Divide and conquer," Simon agrees, a bit too cheerily.

Alex smiles, tosses Simon a ring of keys. "I'll head this way," he says, jerking his thumb at the curving path toward the cages that house the rest of the big cats—a leopard, a panther, Tiki, the old arthritic lion.

Simon nods. Alex doesn't offer any instructions. Simon doesn't ask for any.

The first animal he comes to is a tapir. What in bloody hell is a tapir? The plaque on the fence is no help. Ungulate. Nonruminant. Nocturnal. But is it dangerous? All Simon knows for certain is that it craps like a pig and looks like one too. A pig with a funny nose.

Simon can hear Alex and Dick going about their work. Pock. Pock. Pock. Billie the elephant starts in with her trumpeting again, the poor girl. He blinks away the thought and fires. His hands are steady; his aim is true. The tapir collapses, but doesn't die. Simon gets closer, noses the barrel between the bars and shoots again. The beast takes one final breath and is no more. That does it for the ungulate.

Simon puts down a tree sloth, some pronghorn antelopes and a South African warthog for whom he bears a bit of a grudge; when he was the new man on the job the beast charged out of the brush and very nearly impaled him, the bastard.

Next stop, the aviary. He puts the rifle down and scratches his head. Surely they don't mean for him to shoot the birds. The aviary is nothing more than a massive cage comprising a circular fence with wire netting to keep the birds from flying off. It houses an enormous number of cockatoos and tragopans, beautiful jungle birds. Simon can't shoot them. He won't.

He jogs to the utility shed to grab a pair of bolt cutters. Each cage he passes has a dead animal in it. Bears, apes, giraffes—all dead. It's a terrible sight, like something out of a bad dream. Billie underscores the awfulness with her ceaseless trumpeting.

Simon shimmies up the fence and cuts the netting loose. He makes several trips up and down. It's slow going and after twenty minutes he's still only halfway around. He unlocks the cage and goes inside. The birds chortle, cock their heads, wobble on their perches. His presence makes them nervous. He climbs up, snips another section and pulls it down. A huge flap tears loose. He jumps down, puts his hands on the tree trunk and gives it a fierce shake. One by one the birds drop down under the netting and rise up out of the cage. More come with each shake. They rush past him, great colorful bursts of motion. The rush of their beating wings is deafening, but it does him good to see them leave their talon-scarred perches behind and soar into the sky. It's a symbol for Belfast, he thinks, a symbol of their determination.

But the birds don't go very far. They alight on cages and tree limbs. Some even return to the aviary. They squawk and chortle and chatter at each other.

We're do we go now?
Don't know, mate. Haven't a feckin' clue.
Let's wait for the punter with the birdseed.

A feeling of dread overwhelms Simon. What has he done? He's destroyed the aviary, forced the birds into a world that doesn't want them. He fights back tears, keeps the feeling inside where it sits like an unexploded shell the sappers will never find.

Alex sits on the steps outside his office smoking a fag with a trembly hand. He puts it out when he sees Simon coming and pulls out two more.

"Where's Dick?"

"With Billie."

Alex has the bearing of a man looking ahead. He lives in East Belfast, not far from the shipyards, and he is eager to get back to his family.

"Let's finish this," Alex says. "You with me?"

"Aye."

Alex smiles. It's a grim smile, but it's heartening all the same. Simon would want Alex in his corner any day and he hopes Alex feels the same way about him.

They set off for Billie's paddock in the center of the zoo. It's very quiet, very still, more so than any other time Simon can remember. The animals are dead; the birds have flown away. Even Billie maintains a respectful silence.

"You need me to help clean up tomorrow?" Simon asks.

"Aye."

Alex halts, curses under his breath. Simon looks up to see what the fuss might be. Billie is down. Dick sits by her side, his arm thrown out to embrace her massive head. He's been crying. Alex turns to Simon.

"Did you shoot her?"

"No," Simon says. "I didn't come over here."

They go in through the gate and come out the back of

the paddock where Billie gets her grooming. Dick looks wretched. Gaunt, hollowed out, eyes screaming red.

"She's dead."

"Are ye sure?"

"Aye. I examined her from trunk to tail. No wounds, no bullet holes. Nothing. You can look for yourselves if you like."

Billie looks even more majestic in death than she did in life. Her powerful legs are broken columns, her trunk a curled-up question mark. The folds around the eyes are wet, as are her long, fragile lashes. Can elephants cry? Simon's dying to know, but Da always said not to ask a question if ye can't stand up to the answer. For all her terrific size she was only a wee innocent thing who wasn't looked after properly, and they are the ones to blame.

"There's got to be an explanation," Alex says. "Nothing dies without reason."

"That's not true," Simon summons the courage to say. "They can and they do."

THE PREVIOUS ADVENTURES
OF POPEYE THE SAILOR

"There he sat with his hands reposing on his knees, bald, squat, grey, bristly, recalling a wild boar somehow; and by his side towered an awful, mature, white female."

—Joseph Conrad

He goes by many names. In the Mediterranean he is Iron Arm. In Sweden he is known as Karl Alfred. In Denmark he goes by Skipper Skraek. Here in the Western Pacific he is best known as Father of One Hundred Bastards.

As a young man, Popeye did not display an aptitude for deck seamanship. He did, however, possess an unbridled capacity for violence, and it was violence that sent him to sea when a judge gave him a choice between a berth on a ship and a bunk in a cell. He chose the former. Thus began an auspicious naval career.

*

Popeye was serving as a boatswain's mate on a dilapidated steamer when the ship developed engine trouble and limped into Haiphong for repairs. Popeye went ashore with his mates, drinking as sailors do. Staggering bandy-legged down the boulevard, he noticed a beautiful courtesan smoking on the balcony of a sumptuous pleasure house. She caught his eye, or perhaps he caught hers. It's the oldest story there is. He tried to come up, but an over-muscled goon barred him from entering. Although Popeye's temper was famous from Siam to Palawan, he left without a fight.

In addition to the pair of stock anchors that adorn his massive forearms, Popeye has a portrait of a woman on his upper arm, under which the name "Doan Vien" is inscribed on a stylized banner, fluttering in a wind that never was. On his left shin can be found a dead red rooster, dangling from a noose. Popeye never tires of telling young ladies "I've got a cock that hangs below me knee." Then, that ridiculous laughter.

Popeye was short and scrappy. He weighed just one hundred sixty pounds. He distinguished himself as a man of violence by clotheslining a burly seaman who'd stepped over his sea bag. I can almost see it: Popeye standing over the man, flushed with rage, sputtering nonsense. The bells were ringing, but there was no one in the engine room. He had all his hair then. And both eyes.

Who was Doan Vien? She was my mother. Presume what you like. As for Olive Oyl, I do not have the words to describe how much I loathe that awful woman.

Popeye returned to the pleasure house, shimmied up a drainpipe and climbed the balcony. He parted the billowing curtains and let himself into the courtesan's bedchamber. She recognized Popeye and smiled. He interpreted the gesture as an invitation to a ravishing that she did not resist.

The purpose of an anchor, as any salt will tell you, is to bring a ship to a stop and keep it there.

Popeye and Doan Vien were seen everywhere together. Hotels and restaurants, theaters and teahouses. They made an odd couple. He was ill tempered and rough. She possessed the grace of a swan. Whenever Popeye had to go back to the ship, Doan Vien returned to the pleasure house. This he could not abide. Popeye is an insecure man, tormented by doubts, riddled with apprehension. See how disgracefully he clings to Olive Oyl?

Popeye's past is forever creeping up on him. When he mutters his half-mad asides, is he speaking to his enemies, the army of goons who would bring him down, or is he speaking to me?

To control her, he introduced my mother to opium. He made sure she had enough to smoke when he left her bedchamber each morning. Soon the pipe became more than an accoutrement for managing the quiet time between clients. Within a matter of weeks, it was her master.

*

It is an easy thing to take out an eye.

In the lexicon of tattooing, an anchor symbolizes a search for a home. This is ironic because a home is precisely the opposite of what Popeye was searching for.

What did he see in my mother? A port for his dinghy? A slip for his seed? A vessel that could bear the strain of his ferocious ardor? No. He saw a woman who was handy with a pan and knew a hundred recipes for spinach.

One bright, fine morning that bore a cool breeze from the north, the first suggestion that autumn was coming, Popeye's steamer quit Haiphong for Hong Kong. He left without bidding my mother farewell. You can imagine what became of her.

On those rare occasions when Popeye finds himself between ships he, contrary to popular opinion, does not live in a garbage can. Usually, he finds work as a dogcatcher in San Diego.

Eighteen years after he deserted my mother, Popeye returned to Haiphong. Cavorting in a low class of brothel the likes of which you have never seen before, Popeye stumbled into my mother. She was utterly transformed. Her beauty had dissipated. Her courtly mien wasted by the strain of her relentless need. Predictably, he failed to recognize her, but she knew him in an instant. The lopsided smile. The piss-reek of boiled spinach. That infuriatingly mindless laugh. She came home and told me where he could be found. I waited for him in the alley with a marlin-spike tempered in the fire of my fury. It was not a happy homecoming.

I have inherited my father's anger, that much is true, but he left me no choice. We are what we are. Even he will tell you that.

KESSLER HAS NO LUCKY PANTS

How many pairs of lucky pants does Kessler own?
None.

How many pairs of unlucky pants does Kessler own?
Nine.

Is this bad?
Most definitely. There are days when a certain something extra is required of us and on those certain something extra days we are accustomed to reaching into the closet and finding (on an extra special hanger perhaps?) a pair of lucky pants. But not Kessler. Kessler has no lucky pants. I repeat: Kessler has no lucky pants.

How unlucky are these pants?
One pair of khaki slacks: very unlucky; one pair of navy blue trousers: very unlucky; three pairs of blue denim jeans (baggy, loose, and boot cut, respectively): moderately to

seriously unlucky; one pair of black mesh sweatpants: way unlucky; one pair of green corduroys: mildly unlucky; one pair of camouflage pants: vaguely unlucky considering the situations in which the wearing of camouflage pants is acceptable; one pair of U.S. Navy dress white bellbottoms: mondo, off-the-charts unlucky.

Are the khaki slacks and blue trousers equally unlucky?
More or less.

Why is that?
The khaki slacks and blue trousers are his office pants. Kessler alternates them in the following manner: Monday khaki, Tuesday blue, Wednesday khaki, Thursday blue. Then, the following week: Monday blue, Tuesday khaki, Wednesday blue, Thursday khaki. Fridays, of course, are occasions for casual dress and Kessler wears the same pair of office jeans (boot cut) every Friday. These are the rules. Of the two pairs of unlucky office pants, the blue ones should be considered slightly more unlucky than the khaki, because Kessler spilled some toner on the blue pants and continues to fool himself into thinking that his co-workers don't notice the stain, which is simply not the case as the stain is as plain as a stain can be. Its proximity to the crotch area is doubly unfortunate.

Just how unlucky are these unlucky office pants?
Consider the evidence: Kessler was repeatedly passed over for promotion in these pants. Kessler's frequent requests for an office were denied in these pants. Kessler has been turned down by an absurd number of office temps in these

pants. Kessler was "interrupted" in the bathroom in these pants. Kessler was reprimanded for stealing office supplies in these pants. Kessler's computer has crashed, frozen, jammed, or behaved in an inexplicable manner on numerous occasions while wearing these pants. And so on.

How many times have these unlucky events taken place?
Six, four, nine, two, two, and 676 times, respectively.

Who is this Kessler?
Kessler is the owner of nine pairs of unlucky pants. He works in an office. His job can be characterized as either "going nowhere" or "dead end" depending on his mood. He is excitable, yet largely unsuccessful with women. This is a shame, though certainly not the tragedy he thinks it is. He overestimates his abilities and underestimates those of others. The ensuing discrepancy is often unmanageable.

Is Kessler in the Navy?
No.

Is Kessler a veteran of the Navy?
No. In fact, Kessler experiences a curious mixture of claustrophobia and homophobia whenever he thinks about what life must be like onboard those enormous ships.

Why would someone who is neither a member of the Navy, nor a veteran of the Navy, own a pair of perfectly good white U.S. Navy-issue bellbottoms?
That is a very good question.

Well?
Kessler is very sensitive about his sailor pants. He probably wouldn't like us talking about them. In fact, he's been meaning to get rid of them, but he can't bring himself to throw them away for reasons that are troubling to him, so they remain in his closet, exuding an unlucky aura.

What makes these sailor pants so off-the-charts unlucky?
In 1999 Kessler attended a Halloween costume party. The party was hosted by an office temp with whom Kessler was friendly, but had not yet mustered the courage to ask out, which is a very good thing because she probably would have said no. He attended the party costumed as a sailor, a rare stroke of seemingly good luck as this particular temp, in spite of having her heart broken by a young seaman named Jim she met during Spring Break down in Rosarita, Mexico, many years ago, had a thing for sailors.

What do you mean "thing"?
Irrational attraction.

Does this temp possess any remarkable characteristics?
She does. The temp, whose name is Diane, has a small cross tattooed on the fleshy part of her hand between the thumb and forefinger. She got it when she was just fifteen years old from a meth addict who charged $15 for his services with a homemade gun made from a Walkman motor. Her left leg is slightly longer than the right, but the irregularity has escaped her notice. She once gave a homeless man her entire federal income tax refund—$368—even though she could have used the money to pay her cell

phone bill, which was past due. She has an irrational attraction for sailors. She falls in love very quickly. She is not unattractive. Not in the least.

Was the party a success?
It was. As the hours became small and the guests trickled out the door, Diane asked Kessler to stay. Soon they were kissing, pawing at each other, rutting on the floor.

Was this situation agreeable to both parties?
Very much so.

Why were Kessler and Diane making love on the floor?
Because the bedroom was occupied by Diane's husband, Jared, who had gotten riotously drunk and had passed out cold.

Then what happened?
Kessler's condom ripped, Diane's diaphragm slipped, and a baby was conceived. Of course, Kessler and Diane did not realize this was happening at the time. They were too busy getting drunk (Kessler) and drifting into infatuation (Diane).

It just gets worse and worse, doesn't it?
I'm afraid so.

Where did Kessler get the sailor pants?
From a thrift store. It should be noted that it is almost impossible to acquire lucky pants at a thrift store. In fact, the sailor pants in question were already terrifically

unlucky when Kessler bought them. In this instance they were downright dangerous.

Who did they belong to before Kessler bought them?
They didn't belong to anyone. They belonged to the thrift store.

Who did they belong to before they belonged to the thrift store?
They belonged to a bandy-legged sailor named Jim.

Was this sailor in the habit of breaking young office temps' hearts in Mexico?
As luck would have it, he was.

What are the odds of Jim's sailor pants making it from his seabag in San Diego to Kessler's closet in Los Angeles?
The numbers don't concern us. All that matters is that it happened. Looking back, it seems as if there can be no other outcome. Jim's pants were already around Kessler's ankles at the moment Kessler's sperm was striving to fertilize Diane's egg.

What happened to Jim?
That depends on whether you are referring to little Jimmy, Kessler's toddler son, or Jim the sailor, little Jimmy's psychic progenitor. Little Jimmy lives with his mother, Diane, and his stepfather, Jared, Diane's cuckolded husband.

What happened to Jim the sailor?
It's too terrible to talk about.

What happened to little Jimmy?
Nothing, yet. He's just a toddler.

Did things work out between Kessler and Diane?
They did not. Even though their highly efficient work stations were only a few feet apart, they seldom saw one another. Meeting after work was impossible on account of Jared, who despite being lazy, loutish, and prone to fits of drunkenness was a secretive, suspicious person. So they traded e-mail messages and soon Diane's love metastasized into something strange, the Internet being a cold, sterile place to cultivate a relationship. Each time she saw his bold-faced name glowing in her mailbox, she thought the walls of her chest might collapse. Kessler, however, was having difficulty hurdling the not insignificant obstacle of Diane's marriage to Jared. He was either unwilling or unable to give himself to a woman whose heart was contracted to another. She wrote a lot of e-mails trying to convince him otherwise, but these efforts were largely unsuccessful.

It seems Kessler's bad luck rubbed off on Diane. Was this the case?
We all have our own parcels of luck, good and bad, dispensed in quantifiable units. If you choose to collaborate in the bad luck of another, that is your own choice, your own doing. In this instance, it is not clear whose luck was collaborating with whom.

What's so special about pants?

Nothing. The pants are a convenient metaphor. Luck, however, is real and should not be discounted.

Did Kessler know Diane was pregnant?
He did after she told him.

How did this happen?
Diane convinced Kessler to take a sick day. They went to the beach together. Even though it was June, the weather was balmy and the skies were clogged with clouds. They walked up and down the Santa Monica Pier, holding hands. A pair of artists scribbled their sketches as they passed. The artists had never seen such expressions before. They pressed their sketches into the young lover's hands. He was a dead president in a silk top hat with mad pinwheels for eyes; she was an elfin princess with wings too small to bear her. Then she told him.

How did he take it?
Not well. He asked her if this was good news or bad news. She said she didn't know.

Did he ask her if the baby was his?
To his credit, he did not.

What did he say?
He told her he needed some time, which was a lie. Then Kessler did a terrible thing.

What did he do?

On his way home he called his company's Human Resources Manager and told her Diane was stalking him. He told her about the emails. The Human Resources Manager said she would look into it.

And did she?
You better believe she did.

How many e-mail messages did they exchange?
Diane composed 898 messages to Kessler's 342. Through the cold eye of the Human Resources Manager, the messages appeared to reveal an unprofessionally obsessive woman on the verge of hysteria. Kessler came across as formal and polite, neither encouraging nor discouraging. A more perceptive Human Resources Manager might have read between the lines, sensed Diane's earnestness, Kessler's fear of commitment, but the Human Resources Manager intuited nothing. Diane was only a temp and Kessler was a full-time employee. A bad employee, true, but a full-time employee with a benefits package. The next day, the Human Resources Manager stopped Diane at the front desk and sent her home. The locks had already been changed.

How could Kessler do such a thing?
He was young. Still a child himself. What little he knew of discipline, responsibility, and self-sacrifice frightened him. He suspected the child was Jared's not his, though after he had come home and cleaned his apartment and stood over the trash can picking cobwebs from a broom, he vaguely

recalled standing over Diane's toilet with a broken condom in his hand.

Are you making excuses for Kessler?
I am making excuses for everyone.

What about Diane?
As is so often the case, Diane got what she asked for, but not what she wanted.

And what was that?
A child.

Did Diane tell Jared the baby was his?
She did.

And he believed her?
He did. He had no reason to suspect otherwise. Little Jimmy took after his mother.

Was Diane heartbroken?
She was. After Diane was let go, she went back to the Santa Monica Pier and considered her options. She could try another tactic, make Kessler love her. She could move out, live on her own with her new baby. She could pitch herself off the edge of the pier and drown. It didn't occur to her that she could simply go home, tell Jared she'd been fired, and make him take her out to dinner. She thought of all the reasons why she loved Kessler and quickly reached the conclusion they were dumb and foolish. It all came back to how good he looked in the sailor suit, how much he

reminded her of her first sweetheart, Jim, who had been murdered by dope fiends in an alley behind a Tijuana brothel. She gathered all the artists and demanded they present her with a sketch. A Chinese acrobat performed feats of strength and balance while she waited. Sea breezes tousled her hair. The artists handed over their sketches. This time her wings were strong enough to lift her high in the sky, and her smile outshone the sun.

Is that how the story ends?
No. There is no end. Only more questions, many of which can never be answered. You'd think this would cause more anxiety in the world, but it doesn't. Few seek the kind of closure in life that we demand of stories. We prefer that things be left open-ended by virtue of our children and grandchildren. Most of us are comfortable with this arrangement.

Did Kessler ever see his child?
No.

Never?
He saw a photograph, once, but that is not the same thing.

Where did he see the photograph?
Under the Santa Monica Pier.

What was Kessler doing under the Santa Monica Pier?
Fearing for his life.

Can you elaborate?

While searching for amateur clown porn he'd secreted away on his hard drive, Jared found a file that contained Diane's e-mail correspondence with Kessler. Jared's suspicious nature got the best of him and soon he was sitting on the edge of his seat, reading a charged and spirited email exchange. He did not read much. He did not have to. Jared experienced a series of epiphanies and he figured out that Kessler had knocked up his wife. All of which pointed to a single conclusion: Kessler must die. The Russian nine-millimeter was already loaded and hibernating in the glove compartment. He drove to the office and waited in the parking lot. When Kessler came out he rolled up and told him to get in. Kessler did as he was told. Jared drove to the beach.

Which pair of pants was Kessler wearing?
The blue pants.

The one with the stain?
Yes.

Did Jared know the significance of the Santa Monica Pier?
He did not. Kessler, of course, thought that he did and it gave him a bad feeling, which worsened after Jared stopped, parked, opened the glove compartment he hadn't bothered to lock, and withdrew the semiautomatic.

Was Kessler frightened?
Very.

Was Jared?

Perhaps even more so.

Why is that?
Because Jared loved his wife very much. Because Jimmy was a terrific kid. Because the responsibilities of fatherhood had made Jared less lazy, less loutish, less prone to fits of drunken dereliction. Because he thought he finally understood why his father had abandoned him. Because he felt he was lucky to have the love of a woman like Diane and there was nothing a man like Kessler could do to change that. Because he was sure those fucking sketch artists on the pier would notice two men going down, one coming up.

What did he do?
He told Kessler to get on his knees, reached into his jacket pocket, and produced a photograph of his son, which he handed to Kessler.

Did Kessler take it?
He did.

What did Jared do?
He went home to his family.

What did Kessler do?
He wept.

What did Kessler learn from this?
Absolutely nothing.

What lessons might have Kessler learned?
That nothing is trivial. Appearances matter. The Internet is a poor place for love, corporate cubicles poorer still. A lover's luck, good or bad, is indistinguishable from one's own. A bad decision repeated is not the same bad decision, but another thing altogether, leading to new possibilities for despair. Under no circumstances is it permissible to purchase pants at a thrift store.

What mistaken impressions did Kessler take away from this encounter?
That Jared lacked nerve. That maybe his luck had changed.

Has it?
That remains to be seen.

What can Kessler do to change his luck?
Get some new pants, for starters.

And then?

A TERRIBLE THING
IN A PLACE LIKE THIS

The Floor Boss scampers up the ramp and gives the signal. Pap maneuvers the levers to the iron-spring doors, shunting a terrified heifer into the pens. The Floor Boss presses the snickersnee into my hands. The massive iron sledge is mottled with dried blood and old fear. Its smell is vaguely womanish. I test the snickersnee's weight, measure my grip, swing. The cow's skull collapses, putting me in mind of a sinkhole. The cow settles to the floor, too stunned to know she's dead. The Floor Boss slaps me on the back. *Great Mother of Christ! A son of Cork could not have struck her better!* The florid Irishman hires me on the spot. Pay is a dollar and a half a day.

The cows are brought in six at a time. We work in pairs, with knockers at each end of the rickety catwalk. All day long I bludgeon cows. Their heads make a sound like air escaping a bag held underwater. I work fast, faster than my comrades, and by mid-afternoon I'm knocking down four to their two. Blood-bespattered butchers aproned in glistening oilskins cut their bellies open. Offal tumbles from slashed cavities. Nothing is wasted. Even the blood pooling at the butchers' ankles is swept into a scupper that empties into the sausage works. *This is a factory,* the Floor Boss shouts at no one in particular, *you're not killing cows, you're making meat!*

On my third day at Mackenzie Refrigerator Meats & Sausage a worker falls into the hog vats and a great roar rises up from the floor. Stink McGrew, a veteran knocker with a long gray beard, sets his snickersnee down on the scaffold. *Come on, boyo,* he says to me, *let's go have ourselves a look.* Stink elucidates the finer points of hog slaughter as we make our way across the pens. *They cut 'em open, trammel the carcass and hoist 'em into a vat of boilin' brine. The soup loosens the bristles, makes it easier to scrub 'em off before they're quartered and sent to market. Hogs are hard to kill, boyo. They shit and piss and discharge great quantities of filth when they hit the soup. Mind yourself. That's the last place you'd want to be fallin'.* A throng of curious workers assembles at the edge of the vats. The Floor Boss uncorks a bottle of Chadwick's Unadulterated and passes it to Pap. The worker surfaces, his face swollen, fit to burst. He whips an arm up over the lip of the cauldron as if to hoist himself out, but there's no feeling left in his limbs, his fingers claim no purchase, and he slips back down into the roiling muck. I move to assist but Stink stops me, shaking his head. The Hog Master barks orders at the Italian work party that rushes to get him out. The Floor Boss sermonizes: *Almighty Father, we beg you to bless this low scoundrel, this clumsy, sow-slaughtering scum who has sacrificed himself so gracelessly for Mackenzie Refrigerator Meats & Sausage. Forgive him his pride, this scurrilous social climber, for his pitiful offering of Neapolitan stew. Reared in ignorance, poverty and filth, they know not what they do. Amen.* The Floor Boss bows his head, crosses himself and shouts: *Workers, workers, man your nets and net your man!* The Italians haul him out of the vat like a great fish. His flesh is horribly discolored, the extremities all but cooked.

With two hundred fifty feet of frontage on 42nd Street and another two hundred on Packers Avenue, she stands as stolid as a fortress. The Floor Boss, who helped build the place, swears the factory's blue bricks were shipped from Egypt, cooled in the waters of the Nile in the manner of the Pyramids. To the north, tracks connect by private switch to the Grand Trunk Railway where armed cow pinchers sit astride dusty mustangs, restlessly guarding the freight from anarchic factions within the factory. Darius Birch, the prohibitionist, claims the windows in Mr. Mackenzie's house are barred as a precaution against dynamarchists. Stink tells me there's a Gatling machine gun in the Desplaines Street precinct that was paid for with cattle money. Seany Corker swears Mr. Mackenzie opens the payroll offices on the first Sunday of every month to pay off the Pinkertons, but everybody knows Seany hasn't spent a Sunday sober since the Floor Boss caught him in the sheep corral in his balbriggan underwear, banging away on a forty-pound ewe. At the end of the day the swiftly darkening sky over

Chicago transforms the sparkling abattoir into something more beautiful than it has a right to be.

I live in a rented room in a lodging-house in the south division. Rent is three dollars a week. The proprietor's name is Mrs. Fortunata. Her daughter, Anna, a plump young girl with a game leg, cooks the food. As near as I can tell, there is no Mr. Fortunata in evidence. My room contains a bed, a chipped washbasin and the books I printed with my own hands when I worked as an apprentice in the Bishop's print shop in the Archdiocese of Baltimore. At night I turn the pages and scrutinize the type with a printer's eye, though it would be a mistake to call it reading.

The Floor Boss pulls me off the afternoon shift. He leads me across a secret network of platform planking to a dark and muddy lane behind the sausage works. Three cows stand dumbly in makeshift pens gone shabby with neglect. New England cattlemen size me up like a prime example of horn cattle. The Floor Boss unwraps a new snickersnee with an iron sledge as bright as a diamond. *Three cows. Three blows. Can ye manage it?* I pull on oilskin gloves and go to work. The skull cracks and the blow sends a scalding jet of bile into my eyes. The cattlemen laugh at my clumsiness. Their bloodless derision inoculates me with a wild and reckless fury. I move down the pens a blind berserker, all practiced precision, all reason, gone. The last heifer smells me coming, goes spastic with fear. I bring the snickersnee across the top of the crude stable sidewise like a reaper, crushing the heifer's head against the bricks. She hits the floor without so much as a twitch. One of the cattlemen doubles over, empties his stomach on the red flagstones. The Floor Boss cackles until the color rises in his face. Money spills forth in a silvery flash. The Floor Boss gives me five dollars and the rest of the afternoon off. Although it is several hours before my eyesight is properly restored, I spend the afternoon on a grassy slope on Michigan Avenue watching boats glide over the greasy lake.

The Floor Boss brings me to the decrepit stables behind the sausage works once a week, sometimes more. Sportsmen, politicians, great ladies of the municipality come to wager against my prowess with the snickersnee. I work shirtless one week and am outfitted like a gladiator in heavy leathers the next. Afterwards they take me to beer gardens and saloons where I am declared a champion knocker, a good German. *Not like those filthy insurrectionists!* Word of my exploits filters through Mackenzie's. I am befriended by hog slaughterers and beef butchers alike. Friday evenings Stink and Pap take me to bare-knuckle bouts in the Irish quarter and it takes me the better part of Saturday to feel like myself again, such is their generosity with the Chadwick's. On Sundays I attend church services and temperance meetings with Darius, who warns me against Catholics and the Irish curse. Late one night Pap rousts me out of bed. The Floor Boss waits for me in the street and they take me to a brothel in the Levee. They pay my way and I choose the girl who most resembles Anna. She is a spindly creature easily half my age. In the bedchamber she is willing yet demure; there is no pretense of rapture. Through the thin walls I can hear the Floor Boss striking his boy and I close my ears to their cries.

On Saturdays the workers get drunk. Fights break out on the killing floor. Butchers cavort with the carcasses, spinning their trammeled flanks like gay dancers. Cardsharps use a butchered hog as a gaming table. A pair of Austrians roll a wine keg liberated from a freight car into the sausage works. Outside the rattle of rifle fire can be heard as the cow pinchers try to shoot the ears off a lone bull penned in the stockyards. Throughout the madness the cows come in waves. Their skulls crack open at my feet. Swimming with drink, Stink teeters under the weight of his snickersnee and collapses on the catwalk. I try to get the old man to sit up, and the Floor Boss crawls out from under an Indian blanket. He opens his drawers and pisses through the planking. *Get back to work you fecking anarchists!* Down below the men scatter. I take hold of the filthy Indian blanket to keep the flies off Stink and find a naked Italian boy sucking on his thumb. The Floor Boss staggers about with his desiccated manhood exposed, roaring drunk. At shift's end I find the boy some clothes and bring him to Mrs. Fortunata's.

After church services Darius takes me to a political meeting at the Lagerbier Hall on West Lake Street. A black flag hangs from the podium at the front of the hall. Watchers eye the exit for police and Pinkertons. A bearded, bespectacled man in a black slouch hat addresses a rowdy crowd. *We will not be overpowered nor overawed. They think their stupidity sacred because it is part of their established order. Not so! Force engenders force! Better to die gloriously in the full heat of battle than to be starved to death on fifty cents a day!* The workers' passions are ignited, but they are more interested in the beer barrel at the back of the hall. When the hat is passed a drunken Bohemian Sharpshooter crosses his arms and spits on the floor. Disgusted, Darius gives me the signal to leave. A slender young man of neat appearance whom I'd known back in Baltimore greets us at the exit. Overjoyed, I tell him about my work at Mackenzie's. He congratulates me and urges me to attend a meeting at Turner Hall the following Sunday. Darius creeps toward the door as I take my leave. He twitters with childlike astonishment. *Do you know who that was? Only the most dangerous anarchist in Chicago!*

When Pap gives the signal the knockers climb down from the catwalk. I don't want to leave. The train outside is filled with animals that haven't figured out what is happening to them. There's a question about the billing and the railway inspector won't release the cattle. The cow pinchers double in force. The Floor Boss sends everyone home. I shuffle back to Mrs. Fortunata's. In the alley, a wild dog with a feral, wolf-like countenance noses through the trash. My heart quickens, hot for blood. I unsheathe my knife and creep up on the beast. I slip my hand inside and still its mongrel heart. When it's over, there's a gash under my chin and for reasons that aren't clear to me the animal's entrails are arranged in a steaming blue pile. Broad beams of light shower the alley. I am an angel striding fearlessly through a dream.

*

The Floor Boss sends word I am no longer needed at Mackenzie's. The messenger reassures me it's only a temporary stoppage. The cold creeps up the shaft of the stairwell. I slip back into sleep and dream I am sitting down to dinner with my mother and father in the parlor of a celebrated writer. My father presents him with a new book from his printing house; the leather covers are red like the blood the words will inspire. The meeting is consecrated with cognac. My mother sends me out of the parlor. I chase pigeons in the plaza, their fluttering shadows as majestic as the Dome.

In the street, I clutch the brown paper package that holds the dress I have bought for Anna to my chest, fearful of being jostled, fearful of any contact at all. I marvel at the sight of so many windows thrown open to the cold, the empty frames like the eye sockets of bewitched skulls. A man with flashing eyes approaches. It is my friend from Baltimore. *Come*, he says, *there's something you should see*. He takes me to the offices of the *Arbeiter-Zeitung*—the most radical newspaper in the city. The familiar sights and smells of the printing house leave me shaky. My friend cannot know my father was taken from our home at midnight and hung from a lamppost for printing leaflets critical of Bismarck's anti-socialist law of '78. I stagger forward. He guides me to a cot, begs me to lie in it. I succumb to his kindness. After hours of erratic sleep populated with awful dreams (the Floor Boss in a Kaiser helmet, Anna and the boy strung up in the sausage works), I don't wake so much as rise to the surface of this new reality. A bespectacled fellow reads from a galley sheet, while I look for Anna's package. *We have come to a desperate pass. Political liberty without economic freedom is an empty phrase. Religion, government, and capital are carved from the same piece of wood. The time for parliamentary chatter has passed; the time for revolutionary action has begun! We must pursue the propertied class to their last lurking place and destroy them! We are the lightning! We are the frenzy! Extirpate the wretches! Extirpate them all!*

Work at the factory resumes. The Floor Boss asks me about the long stripe of blood below my chin. He takes my evasion to mean I've been sporting with feisty whores. I contemplate the effects of my snickersnee on an Irish skull. Although I've left explicit instructions with Mrs. Fortunata that the boy is not to leave her sight, he returns to Mackenzie's daily. The boy shadows the Floor Boss. Between shifts I stumble over them coupling in the meat locker. During lunch, Stink frets over my injury. He shakes his head in disapproval. *'Tis a terrible thing in a place like this, boyo.*

I put in as much time on the presses at the *Arbeiter-Zeitung* as my stamina allows, but the long hours in the pens wear me down. I make arrangements for the boy to spend his days with the newspaper sellers where he'll be safe from the Floor Boss's influence. There are days when the keening from the hog vats follows me to the printing house and refuses to go away. Sometimes it's the flies that threaten to overwhelm me, the never-ending drone of a million iridescent wings. The days grow longer and the cloying odor from the filthy lanes weakens my resolve. I tie a wet cloth to my face lest I lose command of my balance and topple into the pens. At shift's end my arms are like dead tubes that can barely manage the sledge. We wash up with crude, foul-smelling soap manufactured with sow fat and I carry the scent of the pens to my room each night until everything I own reeks of Mackenzie's. On bad days the odor is overwhelming and I end up down in the clerk's office sobbing in Darius's arms.

The mechanical doors swing open, the new meat saunters in. One cow stands out from the rest. *Would you look at that one? 'Tis positively massive*, I wait for Stink to comment, but he doesn't say a word. The beast is monstrous. Its thick hide much shaggier than the others'. The creature waddles bear-like into the pens and scratches at the door with great shaggy claws. I peer over the planking for a closer look. The cow's head appears normal enough but the body is all wrong. *What's the matter?* Stink shouts. I want to know if he's ever seen a steer's head on a bear's body before, but I keep my silence. Stink starts a-knocking. His snickersnee drops down on the cows like a pendulum. The cows panic in their pens. Their terror washes over me and breaks with wavelike force. Stink leans breathless on his sledge. *Well are ye going to work or aren't ye?* It takes a dozen blows to put the bear-cow down. Stink offers the Chadwick's he can no longer do without. *Are ye okay? Do ye need a respite?* I refuse the bottle and reassure Stink, but I worry this event will open the door to new concerns.

Without provocation, the police break up a meeting of the Lumber Shover's Union. A scuffle breaks out. The police fire into the assembly, killing one man, injuring dozens more. A worker draped in blood pushes past me. I'm tripped-up by a man being beaten by a pair of policemen and the blows from their puny truncheons rain down on my shoulders. My friend from Baltimore pulls me to my feet, whisks me down the back stairs. Together we sprint through the streets to his dwelling place. His basement apartment has been converted into a workshop. I see coils of fuse, sheet-iron molds, cans of English dynamite. He extracts a composition bomb from the secret bottom of a well-traveled steamer trunk and places it in my hands. Its considerable weight and cool curves feel like history made whole. We race back to the union hall where a dwindling retinue of policemen disperses the stragglers. We're too late. My friend rages, silver eyes agleam. I make no effort to restrain him, but am glad when he takes the bomb from me. *Words are wasted on these men, they respect only deeds*. He holds the bomb up to my face. *Would you sign your name to such a document?* The moon is but a puddle, feeble and dim, next to the metallic fervor blazing in his eyes. *Yes*, I answer, *yes*.

At night the slaughterhouse complicates my dreams. All manner of strange beasts shuffle through the pens: bears, lions, rhinoceri, wolves. Sometimes I pounce from the platform with a curved dagger and hew the flesh with great ferocity. Some nights I move among the stupid beasts in shaggy costume and hack them to bits with an axe. When all my strength forsakes me, I pull on a trap door in the floor and a figure in black rags hands me a bomb with a sputtering fuse. I hurl the machine into the pens and disappear underground. Sometimes I wake breathless and wheezing, the windows in my tiny room thick with moisture, like the insides of a giant lung. Sometimes Anna is there with a damp cloth. If I can't stop screaming she wedges one of the books between my teeth while her mother's silvery shape, silhouetted by the sun rising beyond the curtainless window, watches us from the doorway.

In his boundless greed the Floor Boss installs bleachers behind the sausage works so that as many as a hundred sportsmen may attend. Now when I am summoned with my snickersnee there are six cows instead of three, but they don't look much like cows anymore. All manner of bovine monstrosities prowl these pens. There are cows with the heads of parakeets, baboons, wild boars. Cows that slither on enormous slug-like extremities. Cows with armadillo shells, leopard spots, and scales. Cows with grotesque insect heads that stare at me, hatred flashing in their multiple eyes. Cows that gambol on slender hooves. Cows that beat their wings, scattering sheets of flies in the terminal air. Like Adam, I give them names: uni-cow, yakkopotamus, moo-snake. Then there are those rapacious beasts that resemble no species of bovine I've ever encountered: striped stags with panda heads and fearsome tails, or horrible insect-like mammals that disgorge fleshy eggs all over the pens. I engage in wholesale slaughter with everything that moves.

Late at night when the boy thinks I'm fast asleep, he brings Anna into my room and takes her in a patch of moonlight. The girl's rapture terrifies me. While the boy's corruption

54

of Mrs. Fortunata's daughter is wrong, wanting Anna for myself is certainly worse. Enthralled by the sight of her black hair spread out in wavy relief against the moon-bleached floorboards, I watch, and in my own private way participate in their passion. This is my terrible secret.

Spring brings agitation to the meat factory floor. Mr. Mackenzie cuts wages. The threat of a walk-out gives Mackenzie's masters pause. Darius fears another labor stoppage will necessitate the hiring of scabs, ensuring more violence, more bloodshed. I go with Stink and the others to a rally outside McCormick's Reaper Works. All of the unemployed working men of Chicago are there. Near the speaker's platform, men in sharply angled suits loiter about, conspicuous in the crush of the jobless. A pair of tramps wait for a man smoking a machine-rolled cigarette to drop the butt. The rally goes poorly. The skies darken and many leave early. As the last speaker addresses the crowd the police move in with the order to disperse, clubbing a path through the mob. A police captain lashes his whip at anyone who comes near his buggy. A heavy stone glances off my shoulder, clatters at my feet. Enraged, I pick it up and heave the dead mass into the throng. The noise in the street is like nothing I've ever heard. The workers mount an attack with railroad spikes and stones, but a volley of gunfire quells their charge. A policeman standing close enough to knock his hat off shoots Stink in the chest. A scarlet corsage blossoms in the old man's breast and he goes down quick as a heifer. An axe handle finds its way into my hands and I strike the beefy, walrus-faced murder-er across the bridge of his nose. A bell sounds as if a hundred mechanical doors have flown open at once. Instinct drives me to the foot of a three-legged zebra; a single swipe puts it down. A dark shadow engulfs me as a giant goat-bat takes wing. I knock it out of the air and destroy it. Tiger-rats, panda-dogs, and fanged baboons converge on me. I stun them senseless with my crude sledge. I dispatch a hyena-worm walking upright on human legs, but a gorilla-finch with fearsome claws takes its place. There are too many of them. Reinforcements from the Desplaines Street precinct arrive on foot and by car. I retreat to an alley. Darius is there. He scratches a match along the brick wall and marries the flame to the fuse. He puts the hissing contraption in my hand and disappears. The gibbering horde advances. I curl my fingers around the cool metal and hurl it at the hideous menagerie. There is moment of absolute stasis as I am suffused with a sense of calm that is available to me only after the boy has finished and Anna—the wildest creature yet—crawls across the floor to find me in the dark. Then, oblivion.

Chicago tumbles off its track, plows backward in time, the township reinventing itself in the image of my hometown where socialists and section men, anarchists and incendiaries decorated the lampposts. The capitalist press howls for blood. The police force obliges. Homes are sacked. Unions disbanded. Presses destroyed. But on Lake Michigan the dreamlike movement of triangular sails across the steel horizon tells me Chicago has not yet gone completely mad. I sleep in boats, railway cars, an abandoned apple cart. I pick up bits of offhand conversation and rearrange them in bold printable type. I pass Mrs. Fortunata on her way to market and she doesn't recognize me. Without Mackenzie's I am a blank face in the herd. I race to her home and crash into the kitchen, ravenous with hunger. The boy is there. Anna, too. There is a bowl of soup on the table. *I bought you a dress*, I shout, *but they took it from me!* My senses lead me to the scent of the soup. I tilt the bowl and drain it. Sated, I look for the boy, but he is gone and Anna stands weeping by the window.

The boy picks a curious path through the slums. A mild, irrepressible bubble of shame rises in my throat and stays there as he cuts through the empty Haymarket, but the street has no memory. The boy darts inside a saloon I used to frequent with Stink, but Stink is gone. Why do I have such trouble with that? I watch through the window as the boy navigates his way through the tables like he's been there before. He stops at a place where the Pinkertons sit and whispers in Darius's ear.

My knife sketches a line across the boy's throat. It's not a deep cut, but the blood spurts like ink. The boy doesn't cry out, although I want him to. I stand a massive iron bed frame on end and string him up with a length of rotted rope I found at the wharf. He whimpers and pleads. Gutted, I arrange his organs in neat piles, douse them in lamp oil, and set them aflame to keep the rats at bay. He whimpers, begs forgiveness, tells me Darius was in bed with the Floor Boss from the beginning. This is precisely what I want to hear.

I am going to the gallows. I know it. My jailers know it.

The people of Chicago, such as they are, know it. They think me mad and their low estimation is helped along by my behavior. I can scarcely speak. The festering wound at my throat has ruined my shirt so I scurry about unclothed. I beat my head bloody on the bars and howl at the guards in a language that needs no interpreting. Strange thoughts lurk here. They steal upon me during the lonely hours when even the rats won't have anything to do with me. The events of the past few months, the whole of my experience in Chicago, take on the substance of a dream. I remember elusive fragments only—the brothels, the stockyards, the pens—and the details bring me no anxiety. The only constant is the ceaseless hunger gnawing at my guts. On the eve of my execution I receive a visit from my old, old friend. He stands in the doorway with a bag of oranges, eyes shining. He salutes my courage, my iron will, going on and on how the newspapers of the propertied classes are beginning to editorialize that the horrific working conditions at Mackenzie's surely played a part in my madness. He peels the skin and funnels the fleshy fruit into my mouth. One of the oranges is not right. Its skin comes loose, falls away like the strap on Anna's nightdress, revealing the iron casing of a miniature composition bomb. Louis handles it with practiced delicacy. *Have you ever pondered thus? Would you cheat your fate thus?* He guides it into my mouth. The metal presses against my molars. All anger leaves me. My friend and comrade stands poised, match at the ready. He needs a signal. I take a deep breath, lower my head, and clack my hooves for the Revolution.

PRONTO'S PERSISTENCE

"All alliance depersonalizes; everything that tends to the collective is your death."

—Salvador Dali

Young, ambitious, bristling with determination, Johnny Pronto flipped the tape, donned the headphones and returned his attention to the problem of Salvatore Narciso Dalimante's Cadillac parked outside the old man's favorite restaurant in Tarpon Springs. Mr. Dalimante liked his whitewalls spotless and there was a liberal amount of blood splattered all over the tires.

This is my mother and my father. Questa e mia madre e questo e mio padre.

"Questa e mia madre e questo e mio padre," Johnny repeated, his pronunciation perfect. He enjoyed listening to the instructor's sexy voice. Whenever he played the tapes, his mind veered onto a highway of sex. Darla Duffy, the girl who'd been his Biology II lab partner his final year at high school, figured prominently in those fantasies. Darla had amazing red lips. Although locker room gossip about Darla's lips—where they'd been, what she'd done with them—had prevented him from ever asking her out, Darla's famous lips had been haunting him ever since he bought the tapes. They ruled his appetites, conquered his imagination, filled him with strange urges. They were romance language lips. Huge, glistening pillows of candy skin moving perfectly in synch with the instructor's voice. He started the series ("Speak Italian in Sixty Days!") three weeks ago, and he still hadn't made it through the first cassette.

Big Pete LaRock, a blue-jawed enforcer from Secaucus, New Jersey, scratched his leg.

"Would you look at this," he said to Paulie, a fat man with vaguely froglike features, "the kid must think he's a scholar or something."

"Tell him to stop," Paulie answered, stifling a yawn, "before his brain gets too big for his head."

Excuse me. Is this your son? Scusi. E questo suo figlio?

"Scusi. E questo suo figlio?" Johnny repeated, ignoring the chauffeurs' jibes. When he was done with the tire, he took a step back to inspect his work.

"Get a load of this," Paulie complained, "I'm sitting in the parking lot at Mickey D's this morning. I'm inna car, minding my own business, eating my egg and cheese, when I see these girls inna next car over, smoking a joint, and not some roach they picked out of an ashtray, but a monstrous looking thing, big as a *madura*."

"I got your *madura* right here, Paulie." Pete clamped his enormous hands around a nonexistent bulge halfway down his leg. One of Pete's thumbs was deformed, half the size of a normal one, making the gesture all the more obscene.

"I don't know why it bothered me so much," Paulie continued, "these beautiful young *chicas* throwing their lives away on dangerous drugs, but it did. It bothered me a lot. So I took my shield, you know, the one I took off that cop in Philly—did I ever tell you guys that story?"

"About a hundred times," Pete growled.

"Anyway, I put the badge inna wallet. Walk up on the car. You know how they do. This tough little *chica*, couldn't be a day over sixteen, rolls down the window, joint in hand. I show her the badge. Wave her out of the car. And you know what she does?"

"She blows you."

"Pete, you're making me nauseous," Paulie complained.

"What did she do?" Johnny prodded, wondering if these girls went to Hillsborough High, his old school.

"She pulls a piece on me! A friggin' semi!"

"Jesus!"

"'Back off, perv, or I'll blow your *huevos* off,'" she says to me. What can I do? I get back in the Caddy. Drive away. Probably PCP or something. Maybe formaldehyde."

"Formaldehyde?" Pete asked.

"Yeah, they dip the joint in formaldehyde. Makes 'em do crazy things. Jump offa buildings. Fry babies in skillets. Bite your crank clean off."

"You're lucky you didn't get capped," Pete swaggered. "If they knew who you used to be, you might not be with us this afternoon."

"The hell with you and your used to be," Paulie groaned. "I still get respect."

Johnny shook his head. Back in the day, Paulie Dizoppo was a man of legendary toughness, but you'd never know it now looking at him in his Haggar slacks and a Colonel Custard's Cafeteria golf shirt. These days the only person Paulie frightened was his cardiologist. It seemed to Johnny all guys like Pete and Paulie were good for anymore was humping around, jockeying mobsters, making jokes.

"Look at you," Pete said, "you're a slob. What's to respect?"

Incredibly, the fat mobster started to cry. Johnny eyed the old man distastefully. He'd heard that Paulie had fallen out of a boat back in February. He was conscious when they pulled him over the gunwales, but the general consensus was he hadn't been the same since.

"What you have to go and do that for, Pete?" he complained. "You got him all upset."

"He gets like this sometimes."

"Come on, snap out of it," Johnny urged, "you don't look so good."

"You don't want the boys to see you like this," Pete agreed.

"Screw 'em. Screw 'em all,"

"You don't mean that, Paulie."

The old mobster withdrew an enormous bandanna from his pocket and blew his nose. Pete grunted in relief. Johnny turned his head, looked away. The tire cleaner had dried imperfectly, leaving splotches of matte black against the otherwise shiny surface. He would have to do them again.

"What you say we go on a stakeout tomorrow, see what teen bimbo has to say with a semi rammed up her snatch?"

Paulie laughed and spat on the pavement, a little too close to Mr. Dalimante's Cadillac for Johnny's liking. He studied the mucus: it was green and yellow with a vein of red running down an iridescent fringe like a thing newly hatched. He donned the headphones and started the tape. He dropped a dirty rag over Paulie's chest oyster and crushed it with his foot. Crouched on one knee, he carefully gathered up the old man's expectoration with the blood-stained rag that smelled faintly of new car.

"*Scusi. E questo suo figlio?*" Johnny muttered under his breath as the tape rolled. He walked the rag behind the restaurant to the dumpster and tossed it in. He imagined Darla Duffy in a lab coat, her lips glistening fire engine red. He felt a stirring in his trousers. Johnny checked to make sure he was alone—all clear—and slipped behind the dumpster to practice his Italian.

Tommy Tasca sauntered out of the restaurant. He scratched a match across the stucco and lit a cigar. He belched into his closed fist while Paulie jogged across the lot for Tommy's Eldorado. Later, the fat fuck would call it exercise.

"Great day to be on the water," Pete ventured, a lame attempt to break up the silence.

"Lousy day for golf."

Paulie nosed the Eldorado up to the awning, got out of the car, and opened the door for Tommy. He ran his finger up the side of his oily nose, a gesture he was prone to make when agitated or tense. Pete found something interesting to look at in the clouds as Tommy disappeared inside the car.

Johnny Pronto returned to the front of the restaurant as Tommy's Eldorado pulled away from the curb. A wallet lay in the gutter steeple-wise like an upside down "V."

"Hey!" Johnny shouted, stooping to pick up the wallet. "You dropped your—" but there was no point in continuing. The Caddy cleared the lot and was gone. Pete broke out of his reverie.

"What you got there?"

Johnny turned the thing over in his hand like a jewel.

"Tommy's wallet."

"If I was you, kid, I'd set that thing right back down inna gutter where you found it. Forget you ever touched it."

"And what, sit here for the rest of the afternoon, pretending like I don't see it? That's nuts."

"Suit yourself, but when Tommy asks how come there's half a balloon missing, don't say I didn't tell you."

"I would never—"

"That ain't the point."

Pete returned his gaze to the skies; Johnny's drifted back to the wallet. It was stuffed with cash, but all he could think about were lips, lips, lips.

"What a mind he had, such talent. When I was a young man, I remember reading in the papers about this strange new artist whose name bore a peculiar resemblance to my own. Each time the name Salvador Dali appeared, it grew in size and power. Power over art. Power over the press. Power over the masses. When people talked about him, you could hear the amazement in their voices. How I loved the excitement this man inspired!"

Johnny nodded. Salvador Dali's influence was everywhere he looked in Mr. Dalimante's private dining room at *Nero Aragosta*. Paintings, prints, surrealist objects. Over Mr. Dalimante's chair was a framed photo. "Two guys named Sal," Mr. Dalimante liked to say. The two Sals clinking champagne glasses together before an abomination of grilled shellfish. Johnny's favorite photo showed the confusion etched on the faces of mobsters visiting from New York when Dali had arranged to have the waiters serve them—*voila!*—cooked black telephone with prawns!

"Ah, yes, those were the days," Mr. Dalimante continued. "Now, Salvador Dali is dead and I, his American cousin, in a manner of speaking, am seventy-three years old this month. Seventy-three! What's to become of us, Stevie?"

Stefano "Stevie Two Times" DeStefano shrugged his shoulders and sipped his wine, too bored to care. Mr. Dalimante leaned on his jewel-encrusted cane, nostalgia illuminating a well-traveled path through his memories.

Johnny stifled a yawn. He'd heard it all before. Dali this, Dali that, me and Dali down by the seashore. Quite frankly, it was beginning to irritate him. Three years ago, Mr. Dalimante had promised to teach him the skills he needed to run a work crew. All he had to do was get his driver's license, or so Mr. Dalimante had promised. When his sixteenth birthday came and went, Mr. Dalimante capitulated and instructed the ambitious youth to make the starting squad of his high school football team. It would teach him the value of discipline, working with others, following orders. He did as he was told. Not only did he make the starting squad his sophomore year, he was the only member of the offensive line who didn't give up a sack all season. But it wasn't good enough for the old man who now wanted to see Johnny play both ways. By his senior year, he owned the Hillsborough High record for sacks and tackles and was named All-State Offensive Tackle *and* Defensive End. Now, with graduation already a fading memory, Mr. Dalimante had changed the rules once again. The old man informed him that in order for him to become Mr. Dalimante's disciple in the gangster arts, to learn the secrets of The Bag of Hands, The Shirtsleeve Stiletto, and The Sunken Drum, Johnny must learn to speak Italian. Johnny had just about had it with this wax-on, wax-off bullshit.

"Where were we? Ah, yes. Dali's famous Cadillac. Did you know it was I who procured the Cadillac for Dali? Yes, yes. I wish you could have seen it, Johnny. Al Capone's famous Cadillac. A rotting mannequin rode in the back seat where an interior rainfall had been installed. Dali's wife was a terrific slut. His mind was corrupted with thoughts of disease, filth, and putrefaction. At my suggestion, Dali was to call the piece *The Mists of Syphilis*, but fearing reprisal from the Capone camp, who had recently died a syphilitic madman, Dali renamed the piece at the last moment. It hurt me deeply and we did not talk for months even though I knew in my mind of minds he was right."

Sometimes Johnny wondered if Mr. Dalimante's fits

of hyperbole led him down paths of re-invention. He resisted such impulses. For years he had marveled at the local sportswriters' abilities to turn his blitzes or blocks into feats of superhuman ability. His opponents on the playing field certainly didn't buy it. So where was the percentage?

"Everything excited him. I took him to a Bucs game once."

"You took Salvador Dali to a football game?" Johnny asked.

"Monday Night Football. Dali had a great passion for the game. You should have seen him, Johnny. I was with him when he saw the logo, the old one with the pirate with the long, pointed mustache and a cutlass clenched between his teeth. I thought he was going to have a heart attack. *"It's Dalinian!"* he exclaimed. He told me the logo reminded him of one of his famous self-portraits. You should have seen him, Johnny, he was like a kid. He had to have it all: the pirate costume, the plastic saber, the whole nine yards. Howard Cosell had a ball with it even though the old Jew didn't know Dali from Dick Clark."

Mr. Dalimante drank from a great goblet speckled with mollusks and mermaids—a gift from the great man himself.

Johnny had picked up a lot of information about the surrealist artist over the years, and not all of it was accurate. He'd been meaning to visit the Salvador Dali Museum in St. Petersburg. Nose around, see how much was true. Somehow he'd never made it. In high school, Johnny had written a term paper on Salvador Dali, putting all the stories Mr. Dalimante had told him to use. He got a good grade, but only because his English teacher accepted the piece as a work of fiction. He didn't tell Mr. Dalimante that part. He liked his teacher and didn't want to see her come to any harm.

"I asked Salvador once: 'If you could eat sleep, what would it taste like?' You know what he says? 'White chocolate watermelon candy.' Amazing!"

Mr. Dalimante slurped an oyster.

"Come, Johnny, have some oysters. They're delicious." His eyes twinkled like a child's.

"No thank you, Mr. Dalimante. I've already eaten."

"Well eat again! Embrace your decadence! Stevie?"

Stevie shook his head.

"Do you know what makes me angry, Johnny? Of all Dali's works his most famous piece is *The Persistence of Memory*. Do you know it, Johnny?"

Johnny brightened. "Yeah, I know it. It's the one with the melting clocks."

"No!" the old man shouted, pounding his cane on the floor. "Salvador Dali never painted a melting clock in his entire life! Those are soft watches, Johnny. No melting! Soft! Why is this so hard to understand?"

"How's the Caddy looking?" Stevie interrupted.

"There were some stains in the rear wheel wells. I thought I might go have it spray cleaned."

Stevie Two Times fidgeted in his seat. "I think I ran over an alligator on the highway yesterday. Must have dragged his ass halfway to Miami!"

Stevie laughed. Mr. Dalimante fumed. Johnny dropped his gaze.

"So, Johnny," Stevie blurted, struggling to keep a

straight face, "how's the Italian coming?" Stevie burst into a fit of laughter that yielded a raspy, tubercular cough. Johnny couldn't say if he had ever blushed before, but he did now, and the more the two old men laughed, the deeper he felt the burn. They knew.

"Don't feel bad, kid, at least you can still pitch a tent."

Of course they knew. There were cameras all over the place. Front, back, by the dumpster....

"Mr. Tasca dropped his wallet," Johnny announced, tossing the wallet on the table, "I found it outside."

"Throw it inna bay," Stevie said with a sneer.

Mr. Dalimante shot Stevie a look full of icepicks, and it seemed to Johnny that the old man had just grown older. The excitement that crept into his voice when he reminisced about Dali disappeared.

"Did Pete LaRock mention where Tommy was headed today?"

"We never discuss your itineraries, Mr. Dalimante." This, of course, was the answer the old man was looking for.

"I'm giving you the day off. If you choose to spend it looking for Mr. Tasca, return his wallet, I'm sure he'd be most appreciative."

"I'll do my best, sir."

"For your sake," Mr. Dalimante whispered, "I hope it's better than your Italian."

Johnny felt like a piece of him had just been stowed on a ship and was being bon voyaged from the pier as the gulf between them deepened, such was the disgust in the old man's voice when he had pronounced the word *Italian*.

*

Johnny sailed down Race Track Road, both hands gripping the wheel. His plan had been to motor south on Harrison Avenue, pulling off at the places he knew Tommy liked to go. Now the day was gone, daylight dissipating, and his efforts had turned up nothing. He had been to a strip joint in Crystal Beach, a pool hall in Palm Harbor and a sports bar in Ozona. The bartender at Casa Tamale in Dunedin told him to try the Florida Downs, but Johnny had struck out there, too. No one had seen his man.

Johnny thought he knew shame. His first year on defense, Tony Tasca, Tommy's son and featured tailback for the Pinellas Panthers, ran for over 200 yards, most of it on Johnny's side of the field. Mr. Dalimante was furious with him. It was no secret the old man despised Tasca, whose sole purpose in Florida was to keep an eye on Mr. Dalimante, make sure he stayed sharp. Johnny's dismal performance that day opened the door to endless taunts and jabs from Tommy. Now, here he was, stuck with the task of returning the asshole's wallet.

Johnny pulled off the road and killed the engine. He had to think, tabulate the score. Was it his imagination, or had the men at the track—touts in the clubhouse, trainers in the paddock, professional gamblers everywhere he looked—been excessively tight-lipped about Tommy's whereabouts? Maybe he was going about this all wrong.

Johnny took Mr. Tasca's wallet out of his pocket and opened it. No ID. No credit cards. Just cash. He counted three thousand four hundred sixty three dollars, nearly three and a half balloons. Paulie had told him countless stories about Tommy's exorbitant fecklessness. Tommy was a notorious gambler, a heavy drinker and an extravagant tipper when he was in his cups. Not like Mr. Dalimante, who would send him for the morning paper with fifty cents and expect change.

Johnny drove on, the ghost of a plan beginning to form in his imagination. He wanted to live the life so badly? Here was his chance.

At the Derby Lane Greyhound Track, Johnny valeted the Caddy, tipped the gatekeeper, and bought a program. The sixth race was set to go off. Mid-way down the program he found his dog: *Flaming Lips*. The oddsboard had him going off at 8-1. Johnny laid one hundred to win. He drank a Glenlivet at the bar. He ordered another and walked it down to the grandstand, and watched his dog come in.

"If you see Tommy Tasca," Johnny said, passing a C-note back to the cashier, "tell him Johnny Pronto's looking for him."

Johnny Pronto was officially on a roll. He took his winnings from Derby Lane across the Bay by way of Gandy Bridge to the jai alai fronton where he doubled his roll inside of forty minutes. What next? Poking his head in Skipper's Billiard's he found a sucker and fleeced him for another grand with three consecutive wins at eight ball. He couldn't miss. He stood drinks at the bar, trading jokes with dangerous men. By the time he walked into the Silver Slipper, a Gentleman's Club near the stadium, he'd padded Tommy's wallet to eleven grand. The bouncer ushered him to the VIP room. He'd achieved the easy grace of the well connected. Johnny couldn't wait to see the look in Tommy's face as he counted the thick wad of bills.

Johnny ordered a shot and a beer and sat down when the one and only Darla Duffy, decked out in a red feather boa and scarlet lipstick, took the stage. Johnny laid a C-note on the rail. When her set was over, she came right to him, asked him if he'd like a lap dance. Johnny tossed back his shot and asked Darla if she'd like to make some *real* money.

Many, many years ago on his eighteenth birthday, Tommy Tasca woke from a December nap to discover that his younger sister, Lucia Marie, had taken advantage of their parents' absence by having a sleepover with her friends. Tommy walked into the kitchen and found Smiley, the family cat, nibbling at his untouched birthday cake. This so infuriated Tommy, he pinned the cat to the cutting board he'd made for his mother in woodshop the year before and sawed off Smiley's head with a carving knife. Twenty years later, Tommy could still see the horrified faces of his sister's friends, their stunned expressions the mouth of a dark alley down which he'd crept again and again.

As the years went by, Tommy thought about the incident more and more. His first wife had hated cats. After the disaster of their marriage lay in smoldering ruin, he decided he would never make the mistake of marrying a strong-minded woman again. He re-married inside of eight months, this time to an Iranian woman acquired through an agency referred by one of his poker pals. Initially, he had no complaints. Annya was quiet, subservient, dressed modestly and—surprise, surprise—had a magnificent rack. He loved to watch her get out of bed: a brown flash of aromatic flesh, dark eyes blazing like charcoal in white ash. Spectacular.

Annya gave Tommy twins, Tony and Hallal. When Tony told her two was enough, the house started filling up with cats. He let it slide, but some nights he wondered if he'd ever feel the urge that had overtaken him twenty years before. Inexplicably, cats adored him, and he learned to appreciate their aloof ways. His marriage was saved.

Now he spent most of his time worrying about his sons. Tony, who took after his father, had been charged with sexual assault and had been subsequently suspended from the football team until the hearing. Without football, Tony filled his days with mischief, and just last week Tommy had found Tony down in the basement with one of the cats, a can of kerosene at the ready.

Tommy was even more concerned with Hallal, who'd embraced his mother's faith with creepy conviction and was becoming stranger by the day. Tommy, a lapsed Catholic, blamed Annya. He'd pretty much let her run the household as long as she kept out of his hair. He didn't kick up a fuss when he discovered she'd been teaching them that Iranian jibber-jabber, nor did he squawk when she enrolled Hallal—the smart one—in a special school, but now that the twins were nearly finished with their education, he was beginning to suspect there was a fundamental difference in the way he and Annya viewed their sons' fates.

Tommy had spent the afternoon in the Eldorado, driving around, going nowhere in particular, talking to his lawyers on the phone, planning a strategy for Tony's defense. At four o'clock, his appetite overwhelmed his parental concern and he ordered Paulie to drive over to one of Dalimante's places—Sal's Deli next to the museum in St. Petersburg—for coffee and sandwiches.

73

Paulie came out of the deli with an odd smile plastered to his face.

"What's the matter with you?" Tommy asked, unwrapping a tuna melt.

"Counterman says Johnny Pronto's been all over town, laying out C-notes, asking for you."

"What are you saying, Paulie? This kid calling me out?"

Paulie shrugged and took an enormous bite out of his salami sub. "Impersonating you more like it."

Tommy shifted uncomfortably in his seat. He knew it right then, before his hand drifted to his coat pocket and came up empty, that somehow the kid had lifted his wallet. No, that wasn't right. He'd probably left it in the restaurant and Dalimante had sent Johnny to give it back. Only the kid was dipping in the till, having himself a time. He picked up the phone and dialed his own number. Annya answered on the third ring. In the background, he could hear pan flutes, cymbals, women wailing. Just once he'd like to call home and hear *Wheel of Fortune*.

"Let me talk to Tony."

Annya handed the phone to her son.

"Hey, Pop."

"Hey yourself. Get your brother. I got a job for you."

Johnny coaxed Darla into the back of the Caddy and joined her there. In truth, he didn't care if she slept with him or not, he simply wanted to mash his mouth against the satiny extravagance of those luscious lips. Inexplicably, the feather boa started to shimmer like a thing alive, slithering snakewise off her shoulder, down the slope of her body and

74

coiled around her arm. His hands felt swollen, pregnant with sleep. Did he hit somebody? He must be drunk. Darla wiggled—she was all wiggles—out of her dress. Her skin was dazzlingly pale. The car rocked side to side like a boat riding the swells. Darla danced for him, crawling all over the car, yet she seemed so far away. Where was the girl he wished he had known? *Io non capisco*, he said over and over again as he fell into dreams. *Io non capisco*. But that too, was a lie, for he understood all too well what was happening.

In the dream, Johnny stood on a rocky outcropping, his loose clothes whipped by winds, looking out to sea. A supertanker soundlessly slipped over the curve of earth and disappeared. Two young boys scuffled roughly on the rocks. All around the outcropping the feral shapes of wild dogs appeared, materializing out of crevices in the stone. The boys dove headfirst into the waves and were gone. The hot stink of wild dog washed over him. Small rows of white teeth, silver eyes, gleaming coats. Johnny plunged from the jutting rocks straight down into the Prussian blue. The curs pursued, their black heads abob in the surf, white teeth dripping foam. Johnny propelled himself through the breakwater, into the swells. Out beyond the crest of the next wave more of them were paddling toward him, their growls commingling with the wave noise. Johnny came about and dove. Down he went, down, down, down into the depths, plants aquiver in the green underlight. Row after row of Cadillacs lined the ocean floor like an army of enormous black lobsters. Johnny tadpoled his way up to the car, pressed his face up to the tinted glass for a glimpse of his own bloated dogsbody behind the window.

*

Johnny got out of the car and sat down on a park bench overlooking the boardwalk by the bay. How the hell did he get here? It didn't matter. The wallet was gone. Darla had slipped him a roofie, he blacked out, and now the wallet was irrefutably, unequivocally gone. All he could remember was his terrific disappointment with her crooked lipstick.

A dark blonde wrapped in a white string bikini rocketed past on inline roller skates, leaving behind a whiff of coconut oil.

Johnny felt terrible. His skin warmed over, his clothes rough and ill-fitting. Even his shoes hurt, as if the laces had been tied too tight. He wanted nothing more than to peel off his clothes, run naked into the bay.

Johnny bent over, head splitting, to take off his shoes and socks. He took the laces out and left them dangling over the lip of the trash can. They looked like dried-out earthworms.

"Good idea."

Johnny turned and discovered that he was not alone on the park bench. A dark, bearded homeless man wearing a black and white striped djellaba shared the bench with him. He didn't know what to say. Could he be one of Tommy's? Was it starting already?

The homeless man smiled, exposing a mossy quarry of ruined teeth.

"The feet need to breathe," he said. "They are the most overlooked feature of our bodily landscape."

Johnny looked down at the man's feet, which were bare, startlingly white, almost luminescent. He'd never seen feet quite like these before. They were impossibly clean, like the inside of a sea shell. The man's beard was a hopeless tangle, his teeth genuinely horrible to behold, yet his feet were beautiful. The toes were long and supple, like a lemur's.

"Feet are very sexual. When the women of the Bible sought to bestow the gift of their womanflesh upon the Savior, they ministered to his feet, and he let them."

Johnny looked up, away from the beautiful feet, embarrassed. Jesus Christ, a foot fetishist?

"I apologize. I'm a member of Friends of the Discalced Savior. Do you know our work?"

"No," Johnny grunted, turning away, conscious of his own dirty, callused feet. A swallow alighted on the lip of the trashcan and just as quickly burst into the sky in a great flapping of wings, taking one of his shoe laces with him.

Johnny cursed.

"Look, up there. Do you see them?"

The prophet pointed to a palm tree swaying in the breeze, the tiny fronds turned to and fro, doing a thousand tricks with the light.

"Up high in branches, hugging the trunk. Coconuts."

He was right. High up in the branches a cluster of coconuts sat: furry feline skulls waiting to drop. What the fuck was a coconut tree doing in St. Petersburg?

The prophet stood and removed his filthy djellaba. Underneath he wore black Adidas soccer shorts. He possessed the body of an athlete. He loped gracefully across the boardwalk and circled the tree, scouting the line of his ascent.

A muscular dwarf riding a reclining bicycle whizzed

77

past, a fluorescent orange flag flapping in the breeze.

The prophet scaled the tree with ease. One by one, coconuts dropped to the earth. After four coconuts had fallen, he descended the palm with lightning quickness. He gathered up his coconuts and brought them over to the bench. He huddled for a moment over his djellaba and with a silvery flourish produced a gleaming machete from the dirty folds of the robe.

Johnny swallowed hard.

The prophet sat down again, handing Johnny a coconut. Johnny turned the thing over in his hands like a letter from far away. The prophet held a coconut gently in his hand and swiftly split it open with the machete. He offered half the coconut to Johnny. Johnny accepted. He waited for the prophet to eat, unsure as to how to proceed.

His life, Johnny knew, was over. By night's end he'd be strung up in one of the abandoned cigar factories in Ybor City, begging for his life. The whole gang would be there: Tommy and Paulie, Stefano and Pete, and of course, Mr. Dalimante. If they killed him straight out, they'd cut Johnny up into pieces and line the inside of a fifty-gallon drum with the parts. When they cut open the stomach to ensure that it didn't fill with gas and lift the scuttled drum to the surface of the bay, they'd find pieces of sweet coconut.

The prophet spoke: "Is that your Cadillac?"

"Yes," Johnny answered.

"Even Jesus was not without enemies. Yours appear to have caught up with you."

Johnny was speechless.

"Why don't you come with me? Meet my friends.

Witness our work."

"I don't think so." Johnny mumbled.

"Suit yourself," the prophet said. "While I was up in the tree," he continued, "I saw someone slip under your car. He's still there."

Johnny stood, not knowing what to do. His eyes fell to the machete that lay gleaming on the aluminum bench. The prophet, meeting his gaze for the first time, shrugged.

"Take it."

Johnny picked up the weapon and jogged across the grass to the parking lot where he found not one, but two sets of legs protruding from under the Caddy. He heard voices. They seemed to be arguing. The quibbling ceased as Johnny grabbed their ankles and pulled Tony and Hallal Tasca out from under the car, interrupting the wiring of a sinister-looking bomb. A confused tangle of wires emanated from the deadly device, webbing the twins together. Johnny brought the machete to bear, halving the halfback's huevos. Tony screamed. The other one fumbled about in a suicidal effort to marry two wires together. Johnny sprinted across the lot and back up the hillock to the bench, conscious of the way his naked feet felt in the dewy grass.

"Tell me," Johnny said, plopping the machete down on the bench as the Caddy exploded, a greasy cloud in the morning sky, pieces of fiery debris raining down, igniting the upper branches of the coconut palms, "What is your opinion of Salvador Dali?"

Coconut juice navigated the man's bearded chin, dribbled down his chest, and splashed his thighs.

"Salvador Dali," he replied, "was a tit man."

STILL BEAUTIFUL

April 10

Followed her home last night. Parked just two blocks from the house. Have a permit now, good through September. There are a million ways to get onto her property. Felt brave and walked right up the driveway. If anyone saw me there was nothing in the way I carried myself to suggest I didn't belong there, which in a very real sense I do.

April 17

She makes it so easy for me. Last week I disabled the lights mounted over the garage, and she still hasn't found the time to fix them. She's not exactly a do-it-yourselfer. She leaves the light on in the foyer and it throws out just enough to see. For a week now I've stood in the shadows under the dripping bougainvillea, watched her fumble with her keys.

April 20

Found a grubby little storage area under the house today.

The landlord uses it to store pesticides, leftover paint. Coco probably doesn't even know it's there. It looks locked, and it is, but the screws holding the hinges to the crumbling stucco come right out. The back of the cabinet has rotted away, giving easy access to the crawlspaces under the house. All I have to do is swing the door shut behind me and I'm in.

April 22
Can't believe I didn't think of this sooner. It's better than I ever could have imagined. My whole body tingles with the thrill of being there. So close, so intimate. When she comes home I shudder with breathlessness. I can hear everything she says, feel everything she does. Had my doubts at first, but I can do this. I can make this work.

April 23
Got up early and drove around getting supplies. It was a gorgeous day. The sky was clear and I could see the hills on the other side of the valley, suddenly not so far away. It was the kind of day that makes all the bad ones worthwhile, a day for seeing things clearly.

May 2
Been here three days in a row. It's so much better now that I've furnished the cabinet. Got energy bars, bottled water, even an air mattress with clean sheets. It took a long time to arrange everything, but now the time passes quickly. I thought being here would get to me, force me to find a reason to stay away, but that hasn't happened yet. When she's at work I listen to a little portable radio through my head-

phones. I'm afraid to leave. I might miss something. During the day I listen to her putter around the house, work out, talk to a cat I never knew she had. I try to anticipate what she'll do next. It's spellbinding. She needs me to do this.

May 5

She really is a terrific slut. The parade of men is staggering. She's one of those people who can't handle being alone. Absolutely hates it. After strutting around behind the bar all night long you'd think a little alone time would be just the thing. Not her. Not this one. It absolutely kills me not being able to see them. They say the stupidest things. She only goes for guys she knows she can have. I used to catch her cheating on me with musicians, rent-a-cops, losers from every walk of life. I thought I'd have a problem with this, but I don't. It's comforting to know she hasn't changed, that she's still the same Coco I used to know, that somewhere in her heart there's a special place reserved just for me and me alone.

May 6

Had my first close call today. Banged my head on a joist as she was crossing the living room and it made a hard hollow sound that reverberated throughout the crawl space. She stopped dead in her tracks. *Bubbles? Is that you?* I nearly freaked. The moment passed and she went on doing her thing. She's not exactly what you would call perceptive. That tingling feeling you get when you know someone's watching? She never gets that.

May 18

Thinking about leaving, at least for a little while. Coco's
been gone a week and I have no idea where she is. It's been
raining for days. The cabinet's cold and dank. No matter
what I do bugs keep coming up out of the ground. Hate
them, hate them, hate them. They're so disgusting.
Yesterday I actually lost track of how long I've been down
here. I need to remember to get a mirror. Last night I caught
myself staring at my reflection in the back of a dirty spoon
crusted over with yogurt.

May 19

Came home last night and slept twenty hours straight. My
apartment is so depressing. There's no water, nothing to
eat, just bills and more bills. I've practically moved out.
The things I've left behind make me feel like a failure.
Shattered picture frames. Dingy walls. Even my clothes
make me sad.

May 21

Lots of weird dreams lately. I'm in the back of a van with
a bunch of undercover agents, surrounded by flashy equipment. We listen to Coco getting fucked. She's loud and lov-
ing it. Her moaning is amplified through the speakers so we
can all listen. The men are aroused. I can feel their lust. I
get out of the van, run barefoot to her house with a big
boom microphone on a telescoping rod. The wet grass on
my bare feet is shockingly cold. Stick the microphone in
her window and she starts to scream and scream and
scream. Want to do something to help but I can't transmit,

only listen, and when I pull back the microphone it's crawling with white maggots.

May 25

Okay, I admit it. She's starting to irritate me. The TV, the nonstop techno, the way she talks to Bubbles drives me crazy. The after-hours parties are the worst. Can't leave, can't stay. At night I rush around in the car like a maniac, trying to keep up with her, trying to stay out of her path. Haven't been paying attention on the freeway like I should. When I have to hit the brakes to avoid an accident, part of me wishes they'd fail. I'm almost disappointed when I don't slam into the back of the car ahead of me. Wake up most mornings anxious, wondering where she is. Hate not knowing. That's the weird thing. The longer I stay in the cabinet, the less I know.

May 29

Yesterday was my birthday. No cake, no flowers, no messages on my machine. Nothing.

June 8

Eight days, a new record. I don't think I can do it again. This isn't normal. There's a world out there outside the cabinet. The radio reminds me of this, but the empty chatter means nothing to me. Bubbles keeps me company. I've actually become quite fond of her. She helps me kill the bugs. Still, sometimes I wonder what kind of person could find pleasure in this kind of life. What kind of person have I become?

June 11

She knows. Knocked over my water bottle this afternoon and cursed. Coco was in the kitchen, making her way from the fridge to the counter to open a bottle of Chardonnay, her pre-work routine. It's one of the things about her that still touches me, proof that she isn't so fearless after all, that she needs something to distance herself from the ugliness in her life. Could hear her rummaging through the silverware looking for a corkscrew when I yelled, *Shit!* and she froze. She called for Bubbles and the little beast answered. Coco got down on her knees and called the cat mewling away on my mattress. *Bubbles, can you hear me?* She knows. She has to know.

June 12

She brought someone home last night and fucked him on the kitchen floor. It was horrible, but even as I realized what was happening my hands drifted inside my pants. Couldn't help myself. Like I was in a trance. She talked to me the whole time. *Do you like that? Do you like that you fucker?* She said it over and over again. I came first and when I let out a moan she started pounding the floor with her fists. *You bitch you bitch you bitch!* Left when he hit her. So sick I threw up in the bougainvillea. Happy to see my car, my shitty little beater, but cried all the way home. I can't go back. I won't let myself.

November 15

I've been thinking about Coco a lot lately, so I wasn't all that surprised when I saw her at the gas station tonight. It's been raining on and off and it reminds me of those long summer nights inside the cabinet. The way she looked totally threw me. Not at all glamorous like I remembered her. She looked wet and bedraggled. Lost. Our eyes met across the pumps and she smiled at me. There were things I wanted to say, things I wanted her to say back. I asked her if she was still bartending and she gave me that smile again, that sweet sexpot smile that lets you know she's there for the taking. *You don't know?* she asked, not asking. She thought she was being playful, and I suppose in her own way she was, because that's what she is, what she'll always be. Coco smiled at me one last time as she got in her car and drove away. Took the nozzle out of the tank, screwed the cap on tight, shut the little door. I found a tissue in my purse, dabbed my mascara, and dried my eyes before adjusting the rear-view mirror to see if I am still beautiful.

DICK TRACY ON THE MOON

TRACY GETS A CLUE

Driving down Van Nuys Boulevard, Tracy spotted a gray Mercedes sedan parked in the lot at Morales Scrap & Salvage and pulled over. On the other side of the fence, a dozen wrecks were nosed up against a row of rusting drums. Columns of bald rubber tires towered over the disabled shopping carts and ruined swamp coolers. He remembered the day he watched a Mercedes very much like this one speed away from the Van Nuys courthouse. Alvin Poon, his old nemesis, waved at him from the passenger window. A watch of cops and detectives were taking a smoke break in the magnolia shade just a hundred steps away. Tracy thought about it at least once a day, usually right before lunch, Poon's smile as big as the moon.

Eight years.

Tracy heaved a big-bellied sigh and vaulted over the fence.

The Mercedes sat in a puddle of oil and engine

coolant, waiting for a buyer to shell out a couple grand for its title and the three-inch piece of tin riveted to the dashboard that bore the 17-character vehicle identification number. Buyer junks the wreck and steals another one, same make and model. Switch the title and the VIN and *voila!* Textbook salvage swap.

Tracy recorded the VIN in a little yellow notebook and scrambled over the fence again. He was slower this time, more cautious. What he gained in deliberation he lost in grace, and he tore his pants as he swung his leg over.

He drove to a taco stand on Burbank and wolfed down a burrito loaded with steak, rice, peppers, and cilantro. Delicious. The car radio blared Mariachi music. He turned it up as loud as it would go, keeping time on the steering wheel with his fists. The heavy swell of the accordion seemed to be telling him something.

TEN MINUTES BEFORE LIFT-OFF

In spite of everything they'd put him through (batteries of tests, endless p.t., special diets, new drugs, merciless scrutiny that resulted in the humiliatingly precise determination of his limits), Tracy nearly missed the flight. On the appointed day, he appeared on the launch pad an hour late. Much of his gear was still unfamiliar to him. The shuttle commander came out shaking his head.

"Sorry, Tracy. We can't take you." The astronaut scratched his jaw with the tip of a black government-issue pen. He consulted a schematic scrawled on a dry-erase board angled in such a way that Tracy couldn't see what had been written there.

"There must be some mistake," was all Tracy could manage.

"All full."

Tracy had harbored doubts about going up from the beginning, but he hadn't come so far, endured so much, for this. He snatched the board away from the astronaut and looked it over. The diagram was illegible. All manner of formulae lost in an overlapping scrawl. He pressed down with his thumb and made a space for himself.

"Here," he said, thrusting the board back into the commander's hands.

"Let's get you prepped."

He took Tracy by the elbow, ushered him into the craft, and up he went. Many months later, safely ensconced within Lunar Sub-Station Six, Tracy would remember that day as the happiest of his life. He didn't care if he ever came down.

NOSTALGIA

"What do you miss most?"

"Nothing."

"Nothing? Really?"

"My car. Driving."

A BRIDGE OVER THE RIVER SEINE

Of all the strange and quirky criminals Tracy had faced, none haunted him more than Poon, the smart-alecky little con-man-turned-art-thief he collared late in his career. He was, for Tracy, the one who got away.

Their paths crossed when Poon tried to unload

Vincent van Gogh's *Pont Sur La Seine a Paris*, a painting Poon had stolen from a mansion in Hancock Park. He came by the painting by posing as a gasman, patiently working inside the extravagant house for days before he spirited the painting away.

"And I would have gotten away with it, too," he'd boasted, Tracy remembered. The broker Poon had enlisted to negotiate the sale got picked up on a warrant and spilled everything. Tracy set up the sting himself. After weeks of hard work, he was able to orchestrate a buy at the Crown Plaza Hotel. Poon took the bait. He didn't strike Tracy as much of an art thief. If anything, he resembled the gasman he'd impersonated: small, quiet, of no consequence whatsoever. When he knew his caper had gone sour, Poon ran to the bathroom and hid in the shower.

"My hands are up," he bleated. "Don't shoot!"

TRACY GETS FIT

The first obstacle was his significant girth, which had been characterized on the physical as "tremendous." Rather than forego bacon cheeseburgers and lasagna, he went back on his meds. Soon he was slipping into his old suits again. They were a little dated: the jackets were long, the pants high waisted, the famous snapbrim fedora and trenchcoat borderline ridiculous in the Valley heat, but he didn't care. "A suit is a suit," his father used to say, a nickel cigar clenched in the corner of the illustrator's mouth.

POON CALLING

On Christmas Day, five months after Poon disappeared, he called Tracy on the telephone. Tracy knew who it was before he picked up the phone.

"Tracy?"

"Poon."

"Go stuff it, copper!" he screeched and hung up the phone, that lopsided laugh of his trilling in his ear.

And he nearly did just that. He was so fed up with the job, the way his career had gone south, he considered chucking the whole thing. He was drinking too much, losing too many hours at O'Halloran's, the Chatsworth dive where cops went to drink. He'd emerge from the dank little room on Mariposa Avenue and pass out in his car with the engine running, dozens of parking tickets plastered to his windshield.

THE WORLD

Tracy woke late one Saturday morning and found a shiny silver package in his mailbox. The square envelope bore an Edwards Air Force Base return address. He tore away the wrapper and discovered an invitation printed on a sheet of incredibly lightweight metal.

CONGRATULATIONS!
You, DICK TRACY, have been selected for
lunar assignment!

He took the strange invitation with him to Dottie's to chew it over. After four cups of coffee and a second stack of blueberry pancakes, Tracy dialed the number on his phone, punched in his "Astro Code" and received instructions to report to the base the following Saturday.

SALVAGE SWAP REVISITED

Tracy ran the VIN and discovered the Mercedes was registered to Arthur Eigenbahd, a dentist from Canoga Park who was killed alongside his wife, Eileen, when their Mercedes struck an SUV traveling the wrong way on a median-divided highway. The Eigenbahds were solid citizens, no criminal record. Tracy stopped reading the report. His hunch had gone sour. It was precisely the sort of thing he's come to expect. Another loose thread that didn't piece together with the rest of the fabric. Another lead that went nowhere.

Tracy cross-checked the VIN against a list of totaled vehicles and came up with a match. It had been logged on the scrap list back in 1991 when it was totaled in a head-on collision with a cement mixer. The number had been recorded as a precaution against the day it hit the streets again, rising from the dead like a ghoul, which, it was now apparent, it had.

POON STRIKES AGAIN

On Christmas Eve he received another call from Poon. Tracy sat in his recliner, sipping a jigger of briny scotch.

"What do you want?"

"You know the painting? Pont Sur whatever the fuck?"

"What about it?"

"It's a fake. I got pinched heisting a fugazi. You know what that does to my reputation?"

"It's still grand larceny. They won't reduce your sentence if—"

Poon's laughter filled the earpiece for a full minute before he finally hung up the phone.

And the calls continued.

Each year. Every Christmas.

Poon.

He was usually drunk. Sometimes he was more restrained, sentimental even. On the eighth Christmas, Tracy's last on earth, Poon told Tracy, "I feel like you're part of my family."

Tracy grunted and hung up the phone. He muted an old Veronica Lake flick, *Sullivan's Travels*, and picked at a frozen dinner from Marie Callender's. He knew Poon was still in the Valley, someplace nearby. If Poon was in Chicago, Tampa, Istanbul, he wouldn't bother with the calls. He wanted him to know he was here. Tracy wondered if he passed Poon in the grocery store on a Saturday morning, would he recognize him?

Men kept secrets from themselves; that's why it's possible to know them better than they know themselves. Tracy was that possibility. He was Poon's other.

Rocketing to the moon, he wondered why he hadn't been able to summon the courage to tell Poon he was leaving. Who was on the run from whom?

LUNAR SUB-STATION SIX

The moon was everything they said it would be. The porthole he had to peer through was tiny, the glass impossibly thick. He seldom troubled to look. His new home was easy to maintain. His possessions were as follows: video monitor, kitchen sink (non-operational), microwave, recliner, vacuum toilet, exercise bicycle and, of course, 2-

way wrist radio. The data collected itself. He spent his days watching old movies. Three a day. Sometimes four. Crime dramas, gangster films, westerns. His meals followed a 28-day cycle of pre-prepared dishes, but he found it difficult to stick to the plan. Breakfasts were his favorite so he ate those twice a day, sometimes one right after the other. The entrees were not as good, except for the fried chicken, which was out of this world. He slept when he felt like it. Went weeks without shaving. Even in zero gravity he could tell he was putting the weight back on. His contact with earth was sporadic at best. He could initiate transmissions only in emergencies, and that was fine with him. Each morning he told the computer he felt fine, and it was the truth. He'd never felt better.

2-WAY WRIST RADIO

"Do you believe in ghosts?"
"I believe in you."

THE DENTIST

Hunch or no hunch, Tracy had the Mercedes impounded. He knew there would be those in the department who'd whisper he was doing it to make it look like he was moving forward in the case, but he couldn't stand the thought of the Mercedes on the road again, its ghost resurrected with yet another stolen car.

He stopped by the lot after work, sat on the hood, waited for dark. On the third night it hit him. What if Eigenbahd had been Poon's dentist? The details started to coalesce. Poon on the run. No cash. A perfectly legit

Mercedes. He'd sell it to someone he knew. A square john who'd give him bluebook. Eigenbahd.

"Cap that molar for me, Doc, and I'll knock an extra five hundred off."

He picked up his phone and ordered a sandwich from the deli down the street. Salami. Extra oil.

A COLD TRAIL GETS COLDER

Eigenbahd's appointment book took most of the mysteries away. The entries for "M. Moon" went back as far as 1990 and included one just two months old. He was getting close.

His phone rang. It was Sgt. Reyes from the North Hollywood Detective Division. They had a guy named Poon at the Palomino Motel with a self-inflicted gunshot wound in his head.

"Is he dead?"

"Very. This your guy, Detective?"

Tracy hung up the phone.

Poon's wife, Madeline, came forward, told him everything. Alvin drank heavily, popped pills. She was angry and bitter. He'd used her like he used everyone else, wrecking her credit and ruining her name until there were warrants out for her, too. Paper passing. Credit card fraud. She lived her life under false pretenses. They stayed on the move, going from place to place, apartment to apartment, the next hideout never more than fifteen minutes away from the last. They assumed the identities of friends and relatives. They used credit cards for everything, including hospital stays. Madeline never knew where the cards came from, what was legal, what was not, but Poon couldn't teach her not to care, she insisted.

Then tears.

CHRISTMAS ON THE MOON

"Merry Christmas, copper."

"Poon."

"Why didn't you tell me you were leaving."

"Why didn't you tell me you offed yourself?"

"You knew?"

Tracy clicks off the movie. A Tom Mix western.

"Of course I knew."

"It was getting too hard. You know I was in the hospital?"

"Yeah. Twice."

"Madeline tell you?"

"Yeah."

"You found her?"

"No. She found you."

"Oh. I'd hoped to spare her that."

"Really?"

"Yes. Of course I did."

"You parked your car in front of the motel. She spotted it from the street. You didn't even lock the door."

Tracy turned off the transmitter and started the movie again. Cowboys, horses, bullets evaporating dirt clods. He hit rewind over and over again.

TRACY CLOSES THE CASE

Whenever Tracy ran out of reasons for doing what he did, he took out the file where he kept the photos of the unsolveds. Victims. Innocents. Ghosts. This time, he knew why he was here.

Mr. and Mrs. Brendan MacArthur, original owners of the gray Mercedes now rusting away in the impound lot. They'd been forced from the car on a freeway onramp, shot twice in the head and left for dead. This was back in 1991. His first carjacking case. They were new then. He'd forgotten how ruthless and depraved people could be. They all had.

He thought about the MacArthurs, hanging onto their lives, breath by grisly breath, their blood commingling on the asphalt, running away from them down the onramp, the traffic signal going green and red, green and red, the sharp blast of car horns shattering whatever peace they might have been able to find in the frantic disorder, marveling at the shit-filled sky like it meant something.

In the end, it was Poon who'd found him. Not that it mattered to the MacArthurs. They knew who was to blame. They knew the score. Tracy closed the book, convinced at last that Poon did, too.

LAST CALL

"Can I ask you something?"

Tracy held the 2-way wrist radio to his ear, his heart pounding.

"Yeah?"

"This moon business."

"What about it?"

"Don't you think it's time you came home?"

"Do you realize I'm still in syndication?"

"You got a mother and a brother to go back to," Poon

continued. "A family that worries about you. That's more than a lot of people got. More than my Maddy has."

Tracy pushed himself out of the recliner, the old fears tingling, welcoming him back. He looked through the window at a world greener than he remembered. He thought about hiring a cleaning lady, buying a used convertible, picking out a frame for the certificate that commemorated his thirty years on the force. He still had time. No longer in his favor, but time nonetheless.

The limbs of the avocado tree were stirring, scraping their leaves on the window. He wanted to open it, feel breezes blowing, gooseflesh growing on his forearms, but he'd painted the window shut years ago. There was a screwdriver in the junk drawer in the kitchen, an old buck knife in his nightstand, a claw-end hammer hanging on a peg in the garage—all the tools he needed to break the seal.

RED CAP

The war came quickly to Ilse's village. The notice went up outside the beer hall, and the men gathered to read it. They smoked their pipes and nodded their heads. There was work to be done, and they would do it. It reminded Ilse of the time Herr Schack's barn burned down and the men assembled to discuss how it should be rebuilt.

The men marched into the woods and drilled with wooden rifles, their harsh voices echoing through the trees. It did not take long for Ilse's father to decide a soldier's life was the life for him, and he left his job at the shirt factory to fight for the fatherland. Transports roared into the village with weapons and uniforms. Then, just like that, her father had to go.

"When will you be back?" she asked.

"When the war is over."

"When will that be?"

"Soon, pumpkin. Soon."

Ilse didn't know how her mother felt about this. There

had been no talk of honor, doing one's duty, no tears. The forest seemed empty without the cook fires and the tents, the rowdy songs of the would-be soldiers, the clatter of tin cups.

Each spring new soldiers came looking for recruits. There were no men left so they took the boys. The village came alive with the sound of marching songs as they prepared for the front. They appropriated the stores and slaughtered all the animals, even those that had been used only for milk and eggs. Then, as if in obedience to some unspoken order, they piled in their trucks and drove away. Ilse was beginning to think it was all soldiers were good for: eating everything in sight, moving on.

"Even the field mice follow them when they leave," Ilse's mother said with a laugh, and Ilse's mother seldom laughed.

By the beginning of the fifth winter of the war, it had become a village of women. Ilse and her mother moved to Berlin and shared an apartment with some of the nurses Ilse's mother worked with at the hospital. On Ilse's eleventh birthday, the nurses threw a party and made a big fuss over her. It was wonderful to be around people again even though there wasn't any cake, the women smoked too much, and the windows were all blacked out.

"How long will we stay?" she asked.

"Until the war is over."

"How long will that be?"

"Soon."

Ilse put on the red velvet cap Frau Elke had given to her as a going-away present, even though it was several sizes too big.

"You look lovely," Ursula said.

"It makes me look like a boy," Ilse said.

"Rubbish. There isn't another one like it in the city."

The nurses took turns trying it on, and they showed Ilse how to pin the cap to her hair. She wore it everywhere.

Her mother, who was usually fussy about such things, approved. "It makes it easier to spot you in the shelter."

She found the raids terrifically exciting. Ilse liked the blue lights and bright ceiling, the way the men looked after her when the bombs fell. The constant trips to the bunker fast became a nuisance, but she loved living with the nurses. There always seemed to be someone about: sleeping, smoking, or listening to the wireless. It was like being in a great big family with lots of older sisters and aunts. She scarcely saw her mother, who among all the nurses spent the least amount of time in the apartment. No one ever asked Ilse about her father. It had been years since his last letter. Ilse sensed her mother was hiding something from her. Only after she started feigning sleep did Ilse discover what was really on her mother's mind.

A frontline soldier who had been wounded in the Ardennes was recovering on her mother's ward. Delirious with fever, he'd whispered of horrible atrocities: mothers butchered in front of their children. Soldiers so drunk, they raped with bottles and bayonets. Young girls held down in the snow while the soldiers queued for their turn. He claimed the Russians had taken his manhood in Stalingrad, and each of the nurses had her own idea as to what this meant.

Ilse did not understand what it meant to lose one's manhood. Was this what had happened to her village?

Perhaps this was why the man on the radio urged them on so that the fatherland would not lose its manhood.

Ilse had never known her mother to be afraid—of anyone or anything—but after eavesdropping on the nurses, she insisted on accompanying her mother everywhere. Once her mother set foot in the hospital, Ilse could never know for certain when they'd let her out again, but on those mornings when Ilse woke up to the sound of her mother preparing for her shift, she sprang out of bed and scrambled for her clothes. There was no better feeling than to walk the short distance to the hospital, holding her mother's hand. If she only looked at the very tops of certain buildings and the blue skies above them, it was possible to feel a certain kind of happiness.

When the siren sounded, Ilse went to the shelter alone. She envied the clots of school children huddled together in their assigned areas. Farther away from the exits, men and women stood together, the men smoking, the women clutching their arms. A nurse kissed a soldier and when she saw her mother's handbag dangling from the nurse's elbow, the very same bag with the ripped lining she'd helped her mother mend the night before, she knew her father had come home.

She ran to them, shouting, "Papa! Papa!" and crashed into him so hard she nearly fell down. Before the soldier could put his hands on her shoulders to steady her, she realized she'd made a mistake.

"Ah, you must be Ilse," he said. "I have heard so many things about you."

"Say hello to Hermann, Ilse."

Ilse refused to say hello. If she looked at him, she might smile or cry, and then they would get the wrong idea.

She tore away from the soldier and ran the length of the shelter. The ground shook. The lights dimmed, flickered, and went out. She would have run into the teeth of the attack if the soldiers at the bottom of the stairs hadn't stopped her.

Ilse woke to the sound of whispering. Her mother stood at the telephone with her hat and coat on. The nurses were all huddled at the window. Ilse gathered that someone had followed her mother home from the hospital and she'd summoned her soldier to make him go away. A few minutes later a cheer went up at the window as a car pulled up and took the man away. No one could sleep after that and the nurses drank champagne all night. Her mother's voice cut through their laughter. "Now he will understand the true meaning of rape."

This confused Ilse. She was not yet a woman in the way the nurses were with their complicated undergarments, but she wasn't a child, nor had she thought of herself as one since the day her father had left. Surely, her mother knew this already.

The next day, Hermann presented Ilse with a dog, a feisty little schnauzer named Fritz, and drove Ilse back to the village. She didn't ask how long she'd have to live with Frau Elke. She'd learned not to ask questions that could be answered, "When the war is over."

Ilse mistook the object in the road for a piece of concrete blown from the abandoned sentry post. Then, as Fritz scampered ahead, she saw the sprawled shape of some poor animal run down by a speeding Kübelwagen, but she was wrong on this count, too. As she came closer, it turned into a simple burlap sack, the sort the orchard keepers used. Little Fritz yapped his head off as she gathered the coarse and fraying edges in her hands and looked inside.

Apples. Sweet, delicious apples.

She breathed in their pungent odor. The sack held a sizable number—half a bushel, perhaps. Some of the fruit had begun to spoil. Their skins were bruised where they had jostled one another or sat on the ground, their battered flesh shiny on the outside, soft and sweetly rotten on the inside. She didn't care. She'd eat every bite, and if there were worms, she'd eat them as well.

The first thing to do was get off the road. No one would believe how she came by these apples. They had probably fallen off the back of a truck, but the authorities would call her a thief if they caught her with them. She slung the sack over her shoulder and left the road.

"Come, Fritz," she called, slapping her thigh. A diesel engine rumbled through the haze that hung in the air and webbed everything together. An army truck sputtered along the pitted road. She crouched behind the sentry post, cradling Fritz in her arms. The haze shielded her, made her disappear. It hid buildings, bridges, columns of soldiers. It could hide anything, except the truth.

There was a time when a sack of apples would have been a disappointment. Now it was a treasure. She could almost hear the crunch of the apple as she imagined her teeth sinking into the soft flesh, taste the sweetness of juices bursting in her mouth. Ilse had gotten so thin that when she removed her clothes to bathe, her bones stuck out in ugly ways. But she dared not eat an apple. She knew that once she started she wouldn't stop until she ate herself sick. The proper thing to do was bring the apples to Frau Elke. She would know how to use every bit so that nothing was wasted.

The haze thickened as Ilse went deeper into the woods. The smoke obscured the tops of the trees, and the trunks stood as straight and true as pillars in a church. She could hear Fritz's little legs rustling through the under-growth, and the distant rumble from the city, a sound that was at once both insistent and annoying.

Ilse came to the hunter's path and followed it to the stream. She stopped for a drink. The cold water shocked her lips, felt delicious in her mouth. Fritz watched her, his little tail going back and forth. This was Ilse's favorite place in the forest. If there was a place worth fighting for, surely this was it.

A bough creaked, and when she looked up, she saw a soldier on the other side of the bank, hanging from a tree limb. A sign around his neck read:

DEATH TO DEFEATISTS

The dead soldier seemed relaxed, his head tilted to the side as if to suggest sleep. She'd heard the nurses speak of the dead the way her father talked about failing crops. She crossed the stream, climbed the bank. Her eyes were drawn to the gloves tucked in his belt, the canteen slung over his shoulder. He smelled like horse droppings.

"You there, what are you doing?"

A soldier emerged from the hazy woods. She knew from his uniform that he was an officer. Fritz barked and growled, but kept his distance.

"Come to me, boy."

Ilse was not insulted. There were times when it was better to be taken for a boy instead of a girl, and this was one of them. She didn't know how she knew this, she simply knew.

"What is your name?"

"Hans." It was her father's name, a good name.

"Where are you going?"

"To my grandmother's house."

"What have you got there?"

"Apples."

The officer extended his hand, and Ilse handed the apples over. He peered into the sack. The smell made Ilse lightheaded with hunger.

"You stole these."

"I didn't. I don't even like apples. That's why I'm taking them to my grandmother's."

The officer laughed. "Where does your grandmother live?"

"Upstream."

"Does she live alone?"

"Yes, sir."

"Does she have any neighbors?"

"No, sir."

The officer seemed pleased with this information. He returned the sack to her, removed a bundle of papers, scribbled something with a gold pen, and handed the paper to her. It was a ration card. She'd never seen one like it. She thought of all the things she could buy in the city: eggs and milk and bread and perhaps even some sausages. How Fritz would love that!

"Off with you now. Go get a proper meal in your belly."

Ilse put the card in her pocket, crossed the stream and scurried up the bank. Little white spots danced before her eyes. She saw sunbeams dancing here and there, and a few strange flowers sprouting up out of the new grass. They reminded Ilse of her mother, who loved to arrange the flowers in a blue vase with a chip in it that she managed to hide with a bit of ribbon. She caught her breath and kept running. She ran and ran until her lungs were bursting. She was tired, but she didn't stop. Sometimes Fritz ran ahead, sometimes he lagged behind. They made a game of it and ran all the way to the village as if the Red Army was nipping at their heels.

Ilse spent the night in the abandoned barracks. Many of the windows were broken and a cold wind blew throughout the night. Ilse wrapped herself in a moth-eaten blanket, kept Fritz close, stayed warm. She ate two apples for breakfast and set out for Berlin. A giant cloud hovered over the city, siphoning smoke from a hundred unchecked fires. The smoke was a stifling, unbearable presence that made her throat itch and her eyes water. A gritty film covered her teeth and her hair was filled with dust. All morning long, she spat black phlegm onto the rubble alongside the road.

Then there were the refugees, exhaustion etched into their gaunt faces as they trudged along. Most of the evacuees were women and children traveling on foot, but she saw soldiers on the move as well. All manner of vehicles flooded the road: Kübelwagens and troop transports overflowing with soldiers, and a single black sedan that bore the National Socialist standard in the rear window. The soldiers were in an ugly temper and altercations broke out whenever the horse-drawn carts couldn't be moved out of the way quickly enough. When Fritz's incessant yipping and yapping became hoarse, she gathered him in her arms and carried him.

At the rear of a ragged column of refugees, Ilse saw an old man cutting at the flank of a dead horse that lay in the ditch. As the man worked his knife, the flies that covered the horse rose and fell like a flag flapping in the breeze.

In a field at the edge of the city, boys in Hitler Youth uniforms fooled with a grenade launcher. They clearly didn't know what they were doing. The oldest-looking boy seemed to be roughly Ilse's age, maybe younger, but it was hard to tell because everyone was so thin. He demonstrated for the others how to handle the weapon. He took aim at what she presumed was an imaginary target when a flame burst from the tube and knocked the boy onto the seat of his pants. The missile took out the cornice of a bank with an explosion so loud it startled Ilse and got Fritz barking again. As the dust settled, the boys jumped on their bicycles and pedaled away.

In the city proper, nothing looked the same. Once-familiar landmarks had been boarded up or destroyed. Most roads were strewn with rubble, clogged with debris. Many were impassable. She walked down a strange yet oddly familiar street with a sick feeling in her stomach. She used to live on this street, she realized with a shock. Her mother's apartment had been reduced to a heap of scorched bricks, pulverized masonry, plaster dust. The building was simply gone.

She felt dizzy and set the sack of apples down at her feet. A frog covered in motor oil hopped onto a drainpipe that protruded over a crater filled with murky water. The frog clung to the lip of the pipe, its throat expanding and collapsing as it waited for the right moment to jump. Its legs twitched, the frog flew, and it plopped into the pool with a splash just as a whistling explosive plunged into the building across the street and crashed through all three floors before it detonated. The explosion knocked Ilse backwards into the crater. She lay at the bottom beneath a meter of black water, pinned by the concussive force of the blast. Time seemed to slow down. All she could do was cling to this frozen moment at the edge of inertia, and wait. The hole was dark, and then it wasn't. A great roiling cloud of flame made the water transparent. The frog's silhouette glided gracefully across the pit like a rower in a dream.

Ilse kicked her legs and exploded to the surface, gasping for breath. She grabbed the drainpipe and hauled herself out. Debris from the explosion crashed in the street. A tower of smoke rose into the sky and expanded outward in every direction. Her first thought was of Fritz. Cinders and soot covered his coat, but he appeared unharmed. He climbed onto her lap and licked her chin. He seemed to be barking, but she couldn't hear him. She stood and struggled to orient herself. All around the crater's edge were gooey lumps that gave off the sharp, instantly recognizable aroma of apples baking in an oven.

She lurched to the hospital. Her nose bled, and she could not hear. It seemed as if a blanket of the deepest snow muffled the sounds of the city. A nurse she recognized but didn't know pulled her into the shelter.

"Is my mother alive?" Ilse asked, but she couldn't hear the words out of her own mouth. She kept repeating the question until the nurse pressed her palms to Ilse's face and moved her head up and down.

Yes, yes, yes.

The nurse took her to the aid station where she helped her out of her wet clothes, wrapped her in a blanket, and put her to bed. She tried to remove her cap, but Ilse wouldn't let her. Sleep came quickly, ended even quicker. A nurse shooed her along; they needed the bed. Ilse retrieved her damp clothes that had been left on the floor near the radiator and put them on. The ration card was gone. Voices came through as a hushed murmur, and the panicked throng in the shelter made a sound like a seashell.

When she could no longer feel the bombs' vibrations, she left the shelter and walked to the overcrowded hospital. Inundated with casualties, they wouldn't let her in. She pleaded with the guards, but she couldn't understand their replies. They lost patience with her and turned her away. She had no choice but to turn around and begin the long walk back to the woods. Being deaf was like walking in a fog. The ground she stood upon was firm and clear and looked no different from the place she'd left behind, but the path ahead was hazy and remote, and no matter how long she walked, it was never going to get any clearer.

*

Ilse lifted the latch, and the door swung inward on a well-oiled hinge. Everything in Frau Elke's home was properly looked after.

Frau Elke lay on the bed, and Ilse's first thought was how different she looked without her spectacles. Blood spattered the sheets and headboard. Elke's eyes bulged outward, glassy as a doll's, and her chin pointed at the ceiling.

The officer appeared in the washroom doorway, drying his hands on a white dishtowel. Fritz barked, but the sound was fainter than faint, and Ilse scarcely reacted when the officer withdrew his sidearm and shot him in the head. Even when Fritz fell over, and she saw the blood spurting out of the hole, all she could do was shake her head.

The officer shouted questions at her she could neither hear nor comprehend. He grabbed her by the wrist and led her around the cottage. He jabbed his finger at the table cluttered with coffee cups and saucers. He dragged her over to the stove where bundles of army blankets lay spread out on the floor. She understood Frau Elke had been helping deserters, and Ilse was the one who had led this monster to her.

Ilse twisted her arm free and ran through the open doorway. Something punched her in the shoulder, hot and hard, and she fell sprawling in the dirt. She tried to pick herself up, but she did not have the strength for it. Blood cascaded down her arm. Her little cap lay in the dirt. She crawled to it.

The officer flipped Ilse over onto her back. The anger went out of his face and something else took its place: the meaning of manhood, the meaning of rape.

She couldn't think or move or breathe. She shut her eyes and kept still. Her thoughts began to drift as he tore off her clothes. She was never going to wear complicated undergarments, learn how to smoke, drink champagne. She'd never taste one of Frau Elke's pies or pet poor Fritz again. The tears came. How shameful of her to cry when she didn't know if her mother and father were alive or dead.

The officer stood and yanked his trousers down below his knees. Ilse had nothing to cover her ugly, bony body. A breeze blew, stirring the branches that were beginning to bud. A trio of German soldiers emerged from the dim wood, rifles at the ready. They shouted something at the officer; he shouted back. To Ilse, they were like fish gasping for air. The officer stooped for his gun. The blood leapt from his body and he crumpled to the ground in a heap. The soldiers sprang forward. One of them held the officer down while another cut him open like a sausage. A red cloud spilled from his belly and hovered in the cool forest twilight. Within the cloud, Ilse saw the faces of Frau Elke, the soldier she'd found hanging by the stream, all the men and women the officer had murdered. One of the soldiers lifted Ilse up and carried her inside the house. Sunlight spilled through the windows and an apple pie cooled on the sill. Her mother sat at the table arranging flowers in a bright blue vase. She yearned to go to her, but Ilse's father held her tight, pressed his lips to her cheek, whispered the words she had waited so long to hear.

Wake up, little one. The war is over.

THE EGGMAN

SENSITIVITY TRAINING

Contrary to what you might think, I don't blame Rumi, the boss' wife, or any of the hundred women who have ruined me. No, I blame Constance Careful, motivational speaker extraordinaire. Without her, I never would have become The Eggman.

It started after an unpleasant exchange at the company picnic where I told a couple of off-color jokes to the supervisor's wife. Apparently, neither she nor her clenched-ass husband found my jokes in good taste. The office was abuzz for weeks with accounts of how I'd told her an anatomically correct version of a dick joke, a claim I deny, although it sounds like something I'd do. Human resources "strongly recommended" I attend Sensitivity Training. Rumi, my wife, was thrilled.

It's difficult for me to be objective, that much I will allow, but on the subject of Sensitivity Training, I consider myself something of an expert. Unbeknownst to Rumi, I'd been carrying on an affair with a woman who made her living on the self-help seminar circuit. She wasn't attractive by any means. She was stoop-shouldered and mousey-looking, but boy could she talk. When our time together had nearly run its course, I was convinced Ms. Constance Careful was a walking, talking catalog of neuroses who had no business dispensing advice to people with real problems. Imagine my horror as I reported for Sensitivity Training at the Ronald Reagan Room at the Newport Beach Hilton and discovered my soon-to-be jilted lover at the podium.

I tried to get out of it, of course, talk Constance into signing off on the paperwork during one of our private sessions in her room upstairs. I even held out on her, refused to give up the goods, but she knew I was bluffing and our lovemaking that afternoon was ardent and full of danger.

The seminar (Lesson #1: "Eggs Are People Too") was already underway when I took my seat. Men in white jumpsuits passed out hard-boiled eggs and magic markers while my secret lover gave us these inspiring words:

"The egg is a symbol of life. The miracle from which all creation springs. To hold an egg is to hold one of life's most unfathomable mysteries. The inscrutable of inscrutables. God's most magnificent contradiction."

Constance held an egg up for us all to see. The color was rising in her cheeks. Someone coughed. Another cleared his throat. The guy next to me took the cap off his magic marker and inhaled. The familiar odor brought me back a couple decades. Constance prattled on.

"But the source is not the source. For life to thrive within this tiny engine, it needs warmth and attention and kindness and love, things it is powerless to provide. Without them, the egg turns foul, collapses on itself and dies. Life needs love to live. Say it with me."

I went through the motions while the rest of her sorry flock obliged, but Ms. Careful made us repeat the words until she had us raving like high school kids at a pep rally.

"What a bunch of hooey," I muttered to the guy next to me, but he didn't hear me. His eyes were glazed over, his face taut with rapture. I scooted my chair away. Constance pounded the podium, trembling with the power of her good intentions. A wild creature in sensible shoes.

"The power of love is to bring life to where none exists. Love is that power. The X-factor in our daily equations. I want you all to take your magic marker and your egg and bring life to the blank face of creation. Do it now."

Constance walked the aisles, offering praise and encouragement.

"Put your own stamp on it. Personalize it. Remember, life needs love to live. How are we coming along here?"

She stood over me, eyes sparkling. Her chest rose and fell. She was in full bloom. Creation's willing mistress.

"I don't know how," I said, my mouth suddenly dry.

"Let me help you."

Constance got down on her knees and took the egg from me. She uncapped the marker and drew two perfect eyes, a perfect nose, perfect lips. When she blew the wet ink dry, I very nearly fell out of my chair.

"Here, give it a try."

The marker, which Constance had used with such efficient grace, felt clumsy in my hand.

"I can't. I'll just fuck it up."

She came closer. I could smell her perfume, count the links in her necklace. The air conditioning in the Ronald Reagan Room roared like the steam plant of an ocean liner. Ms. Careful's tongue darted in and out of my ear.

"You can't hurt it," she whispered. "It's already dead."

EGGMAN AT HOME

Sunday morning, March 9, early spring. A time for rebirth and all the shit that goes with it, but with a triple header on the tube and the NCAA Men's Basketball Tournament selection show on ESPN, it's quite possibly the one day of the year when the whole country is going apeshit over basketball. I get up from the table, put my dishes in the sink, slide my keys across the counter into my pocket.

"You know something," Rumi says, raising the napkin to her lips, "you haven't changed a bit."

Here we go again. Another installment of "Who Gets The Last Word." Even though I'm on my way out the door, places to go, horses to handicap, I can't let it pass. I say something juvenile. Rumi answers back. Like a couple of over-rehearsed actors, we volley back and forth, waiting for the other to up the ante, kick start this made-for-television drama into late-night cable action. I pound on the kitchen table, making the silverware do that edgy dance they do. Rumiko goes a little batty, rages through the house slamming doors, rattling china, knocking the wall hangings atilt. Finally, she shuts herself in the spare bedroom where she keeps the dope and the photo albums she thinks I don't know about. I listen for the sound of the lock scraping into place, and just like that I'm shutout again, like at the track only worse because at least the cashiers at the mutuels windows will talk to you if you look like you need talking to, commiserate with you even, bemoan your bad fortune and shitty luck that only seems to worsen by the hour.

Rumi says I don't remember things, but I remember plenty, like the first time I sank the eight ball on the break at the old Knights of Columbus building. I remember when I won big at craps in Vegas and the bellhop at the Sands tried to blow me in the elevator. I remember the day Magic Johnson announced to the world he had the AIDS. Those kinds of things I remember. For the life of me though, I can't recall what kind of car I learned to drive on, or what the weather was like on the day I was married, or the name of the girl I lost my virginity to (although I'm positive she had red hair and that I haven't had it since). I'm finally on my way, backing out of the driveway, when it hits me: March 9 = Rumi's birthday = oh fuck. Naturally, I go straight to the florist.

Talk about Sad-Sack Central. The place is packed with slack-jawed simps, walking around the store with hands in their pockets, picking through overpriced arrangements put together by acne-ravaged teenagers who wear their indifference to love like a dirty apron. I get the fuck out of there. Try another florist. And another after that. Whatever reasons I might have had for dumping forty bucks on a bunch of ribbons and twigs starts to slip away. I'm almost out of there when I see this bucket full of yellow tulips rimmed in orange and red like a thing aflame. My heart quickens as I pick one. I picture giving Rumi this magnificent flower, this vibrant, thriving symbol of the fiery core of my love. She'll know it's every good thing

I've ever felt about her since the moment I first laid eyes on her at Dodger Stadium and followed her to her seat in the loge with my binoculars. I'll never forget the way the world fell out of focus around her. Her hair all silky and dark, her face a composite of delicacies. She laughed at something her girlfriend said and my heart surged in my breast like a dog mounting another dog. I memorized every line, every shadow. I bumped into her in the beer line and put her in my life the way a jeweler sets a diamond in silver.

EGGMAN AT THE BAR

I'm not in the place two seconds when this asshole sitting next to me says: "If you had a penis growing out of your forehead, how big would it be?"

The cracked leather under my ass is still cold to the touch, my Bloody Mary a thing unmade, and it's already starting. Dim eyes down the length of the bar swivel in our direction, the ripple effect of their cattle-prodded curiosity is like an old television warming up, weird distortions yielding to something banal and dull. Morning drinkers drunk on their own hilarity are not my idea of entertainment.

"I don't know."

"And you never would," he cackles, "cuz yer balls would be hanging in your eyes!" Mr. Hilarious-at-10-o'clock-in-the-morning pounds the bar.

I feign laughter, get a cigarette going, but he won't let up. He glares at the tulip perched in a water glass atop the bar.

"Nice flower."

"Go fuck yourself."

Hilarious jumps off his stool, cracks a bottle of Coors on the lip of the bar. Beer drools out of the neck, dribbles on his shoes, but the bottle doesn't break. The bar goes quiet. Hilarious tries again. This time the bottle shatters in his hand and he starts to howl. He staggers around, knocking over drinks. The patrons shout. An enormous Mexican cook emerges from the kitchen gripping a ladle with a scooper on it as big as a wrecking ball. The drunk begins to whimper and cry, suddenly not so funny anymore. He holds his bloodied hand out in front of him like a beggar.

After they throw him out, I ask the bartender to get the Lakers game on the television and she looks at me like I got eight brains and none of them are working right. She leans across the bar, the gap in her blouse growing wider as her breasts settle on the ancient wood.

"Is that for me?"

"Wife."

"Oh, a romantic. What did you do?"

"Nothing."

"You must have done something bad. Are you a bad boy?"

"The worst."

I busy myself with my drink while she works the remote. The Lakers swim on the screen, game already in progress. The players look like they're sleepwalking, going through the motions. Two, three, four trips down the floor and nobody scores. One drink turns to two, half time comes and goes, and "just-one-more" becomes my mantra for the remainder of the game. The Lakers pull off an incredible comeback but the victory feels like a defeat, another dismal failure of the imagination, a weak nut.

MORE NAGS

Indecision cripples, action exhilarates, and I didn't learn that in a Sensitivity Seminar.

It's unseasonably warm. Earthquake weather. My car, badly in need of an $800 tune-up, quits on me as I pull into a parking spot at the racetrack at Hollywood Park in the City of Champions. With the tulip clenched in my teeth, I look like a Dutch swashbuckler. I leave the keys in the ignition and hustle to the turnstile.

First race. Two minutes to post. Just enough time to get in line and throw out some names. Two horses catch my eye: *Sunny Side Up* and *Which Came First?* I lay forty dollars on an exacta box. The cashier eyeballs the tulip, says nothing. Sure enough, my nags come in, but that's just the beginning. Long shots, trifectas, daily doubles. You name it. Everything goes my way. Cool breezes keep the heat at bay, but the tulip wilts, breakage in the stem. I keep thinking about Rumi, locked in the guest bedroom, listening to Leon Redbone, getting high and trying on hats. I'm winning, but I bet carelessly, missing opportunities to make some real money. I try to gather my thoughts, narrow my focus, but it's no use. I keep my head down and keep drinking, relying on my good fortune—this wayward boon—to win the day.

Inside the Turf Club, I hear my name being called and who should it be but my old friend Franky Mac, a pitiful sportsman with a predilection for virgins. Disease control, he calls it. His eyes tell the story. Franky's in trouble. Not Sunday-afternoon-at-the-track trouble, but real trouble. He knocked up a little Mexican girl, he tells me, a butcher's daughter with lots of brothers, and she wants to keep the baby. He needs a grand to pay off a doctor who'll induce a miscarriage when she comes in for an examination. I give him a hundred and a sure thing in the eighth.

"Nice flower," he says.

"I hope those hombres lop your nuts off."

I wander outside. High up in the grandstand a lone woman stares at the sun. A possible jumper. There's something familiar about the way she stands, the way she sweeps her glistening hair back with her hand. I'm suddenly sick of it all, the too-bright sun, the welfare population at the rails, the indifference of the cashiers at the mutuels windows, the frantic look in the horses' eyes as they roar past the wire. A strong breeze catches the top of the beer bottle angled just so in my hand, making it moan like a monstrous whore. I slam my hand over the top, a magician stoppering an evil djinn.

I drive past Psycho Nudes by the airport, wondering what the dancers will look like, but I end up at Muldoon's on La Cienega, a place as gloomy as my mood. I set the tulip, water glass and all, on the bar, resolving to deck the first person to send any static my way. Franky Mac comes roaring into the bar with a fresh hooker on one elbow, a used-up skag on the other. Franky flush? To the rest of the bar this is news, but I know the score.

Franky makes a big show of his roll and quickly buys the house a round, a gesture that never goes unappreciated at Muldoon's. Franky Mac tells the story of how I gave him the tip and the old-timers at the bar ease up a little bit, recalling the days when Franky's brothers used to roll in after robbing a liquor store to drink up the take, bragging about it to anyone who would listen. Franky was a pervert and a braggart, but to his credit he never felt the compulsion toward random acts of thuggery like the rest of his brood. He corners a late arrival and starts blathering away like an idiot. The women, strangers to one another, drink up Franky's money, throwing back shots of Wild Turkey with wild enthusiasm.

In an age when everyone believes they have something important to say, listening amounts to what most people do while they search for a relevant topic to interrupt you with. Some people are talkers. Take Constance for example. Talk until she's blue in the face. Not me, I'm a listener. Rumi too. Sometimes hours, entire days drift by in total silence.

After listening to Cindy, the younger of the two whores, and Danielle, barely seventeen, for a few rounds, I decide that Franky Mac has bitten off more than he can chew, a feeling I suspect Cindy and Danielle share. Tired of spending his money on people whose low opinion of him is forever cemented in the lore of Muldoon's, Franky lurches over to the table to grope the girls.

"Who wants to dance?" he asks, hiccupping and slurring.

"There's no music," Cindy says.

"Dance with him," Danielle giggles, but Cindy is so drunk she can barely walk. Cindy throws her head back and laughs—the party girl's last stand. Franky grabs Cindy around the waist and pulls her into the space between the pool tables where the barlight is bright and unforgiving. Franky takes her roughly by the wrist and spins her. Cindy goes limp, a burden to what little grace Franky possesses. He curses as he pulls Cindy to her feet and slings her over his shoulder. Franky spins round and round and round. Cindy laughs like the little girl she is. Eventually, inevitably you might say, Franky slips and falls in a tangle of limbs. For a moment no one moves. Then, with inexorable slowness, Cindy stirs and starts going through Franky's pockets.

Danielle smiles. Her fingernails dance on my hands. I shiver, suddenly cold.

"Tell me," she says, smiling through horrible teeth, "Why do you beat your wife?"

CONSIDER YOURSELF EGGUCATED

I never would have guessed that carrying an egg around with me everywhere I went (Lesson #2: Eggspanding Your Horizons) would have such a profound impact on my life. All my friends thought I'd gone soft. I'd walk into a joint, set the little whatnot down on the bar, and listen to them snickering behind my back.

The weird thing is Constance was right. I actually learned to like the little fella. I hung an onion sack from the rear-view mirror so he could ride with me up front. I even took to reading the sports pages to him. Maybe I did go a little daffy. Bartender friend of mine said it was because I didn't have any children around the house. I asked Constance about it and she agreed in that cold, nonsensical way of hers that made me certain I'd never tell her that Rumi and I couldn't have kids and never would.

When Constance dumped me, I took it out on the egg, my constant companion. First, I gave the egg a mustache, to masculinize the little fucker. Pleased with the results, I drew some eyebrows, only they didn't come out right. The left eyebrow was bushier than the right, distorting the egg's symmetry. I kept extending the eyebrows until they looked like big black worms. Finally, I turned the eyebrows into sunglasses, obliterating the eyes altogether. Before I knew it, my egg was sporting a pointy little beard and—what the hell—a cigarette too. It looked like a beatnik and I took to addressing it in a French accent. *Ah Frenchy, it eez a beautiful day for zee races, n'est pas?*

Frenchy and I became fast friends and the friendship spilled over into my relationship with Rumi. We talked during meals again. Watched TV together. We even went to a Dodger game. Just the three of us.

I thought about Constance less and less. I had to hand it to her: the egg was a good call. I wondered what else she had been right about.

Then one day, one of the regulars at Muldoon's decided to play a joke on me. When nature called, I left Frenchy on the bar. Imagine my surprise when I came back from the little sailor's room and discovered a tiny little plate of scrambled eggs at my place at the bar, sour steam wrinkling my eyes.

I don't know if I can rightly explain how I felt at that particular moment, but I learned my lesson: sensitivity is exposure, a vulnerability that leaves you as fragile as the day you were born. Frenchy was not my friend. Hell, I knew that. Sitting over the annihilated embryo, I understood all too well it wasn't Frenchy who was destroyed that day. The desire to make men sensitive, subservient in spirit and deed to the will of women, is nothing more than a plot to emasculate us. Let's face it, it wasn't Frenchy's ooey, gooey inside I'd tried to come to terms with, but the friendly face painted on its brittle shell. And so it is with women, and you can't unscramble them. I went to one of my former lover's seminars to tell her all about this new idea I'd hatched.

"What's so great about an egg anyway?" I shouted at the assembly, my voice too loud as I swayed in the center aisle of the conference room.

Constance did not go down without a fight. "Eggs are beautiful. Eggs are perfect. Eggs are fragile and strong in the same instant." If there was one thing she never failed to draw inspiration from, it was the almighty egg.

"That's a load of crap," I told her, "I can think of lots of reasons why it would suck to be an egg."

I held my breath. Ms. Careful looked me over. For a moment, I saw what she saw—what they all saw: a gambler with a rap sheet about to self-destruct. I might as well have been holding a battered can of Pabst in one hand and a bomb with a sputtering fuse in the other.

"Name one," she said.

I exhaled. Victory was close at hand. "Your father's a cock. Your mother's a dumb cluck and an easy lay. It takes three minutes to get hard and you only get laid once."

I had them rolling in the aisles. Not everyone laughed, just the ones who didn't want to be there, which was most of them. Hell, even some of the women laughed. Ms. Careful had met her match and the whole room knew it. She showed me the door. Gave me the old heave ho. I was a gentleman about it. I didn't ask for my money back, didn't put on a show. I even refrained from the old if-you-

knew-Constance-like-I-knew-Constance routine I'd prepared. I simply stood up from my seat and addressed my
fellow sensitivity trainees:

"There's a Hooter's across the street. Who's with me?"

I'll be damned if every swinging dick in the room did-
n't stand up. Okay, so their women pulled most of them
back down to their seats, but the men who'd wisely left
their better halves at home stayed standing, and we made a
noisy ruckus as we left. Proudest moment of my life. In the
bar, they took a picture of me and my converts, and I'm
told it's still hanging there today, right next to Shaquille
O'Neal's. One small step for assholeishness; one enor-
mously humiliating moment for a woman who had it
coming.

PSYCHO NUDES

The first thing you notice is the music. It fills the
room. Then there's the darkness, the chairs, women everywhere you look. Wicked women, beautiful strangers, crazy
ladies—just like the sign says. The dancer blushes when I
show her my flower even though it isn't much to look at
any more. Flowers. Fruiting bodies. Sex organs of the plant
world. The dancer winks at me and only an idiot would
miss the message encrypted in the torpid descent of those
lashes. She oozes closer, introducing a thousand possibilities in the curve of her lips, possibilities ten folded by the
light grace of her hand on my shoulder. I remember the first
time I held a buttercup under Rumi's chin. Silly romantic
bullshit, only it fucking worked: a splash of gold appeared,
like some kind of spell authenticating my intentions. Only
it's so dark and loud in here I can barely stay in my chair.

The world goes by in a wobbly rush. The dancer grinds away, plays with her hair.

"What's your name?"

"You already asked me."

"Tell me again."

"Santana."

"That's a beautiful name."

"That's what you said the last time."

I hold the tulip up to Santana's face, a face made to be compared to such things, and all her life no one told her. She pushes me back in my chair, knocking over my drink. Rumi's always knocking things over, breaking things, smashing them to pieces. I swear she does it on purpose. Dropped a jar of spaghetti sauce in the middle of the kitchen because she knew I'd get angry, knew what would happen next. Christ almighty what I did to her. Spent the night in jail even though I took her to the emergency room and didn't have a drop of liquor in me. The cops looked at me and looked at her and looked at me, fire in their eyes, their cop hearts aflame. "See?!" I tried to tell them, "See?!" but they didn't see, they missed the point altogether. Same song, different dancer. The new girl settles on my thighs, a limber goddess in a pink bikini. She shakes her hair in my face, each perfumed point of contact a tiny miracle. I hold on to the flower so tight my fingernails tear into the fleshy stem. The crumpled bar rag at my feet is like a used-up bandage hardening in the wastebasket. Another dancer knee-walks center stage. The wall of mirrors buckles and swims in the play of lights. Handprints, tiny dead spots in the strobe, resist the crazy motion, retaining their oily whatness. The strobe persists, keeping time with my fists on the door of the guest bedroom. A camera flashes, documenting the limits of Rumi's endurance. She slides a Polaroid through the crack and the tiny portrait makes me weep like a baby. The dancer brushes the damp hair from my eyes sensing all is not well here. I show her the flower. She's wary of me, maybe even a little afraid, but not without sympathy, just the way I like it.

"Here," I say, "this is for you."

BRAINS FOR BENGO

Bengo Action Tiger can crouch, crawl, and pounce. It has motion detectors in its eyes, so it can attack you in the dark. Bengo isn't plastic. It's soft, like a stuffed animal. I mean, it *is* a stuffed animal. When I pick it up, it's heavy and I can totally tell there's stuff going on inside. Bengo looks like one of the toys my sister, Lisa, used to collect before the operation.

Dad is in Thailand. He doesn't live with us anymore, but when he's in town we spend the last weekend of the month at his house in Malibu. He sends us postcards from dirty-sounding places like Bangkok and Phuket. He's in the import/export business, but if you ask Mom she'll say he's "in the business of getting his rocks off," and the way she says it makes that sound dirty, too.

Mom went to the islands. There's a picture of her at her favorite hotel on the wall near the bar. She's wearing a bathing suit and a big straw hat. She's got a drink in one hand and a pineapple in the other. She's laughing so hard her eyes are little squints. It's my favorite picture of her. It's my favorite picture period.

I can't lie. I got the idea watching the *Abbott & Costello Meet Frankenstein* DVD. This evil scientist woman wants to take out Frankenstein's brains and put Costello's in to make the monster more obedient. It's pretty funny for an old movie. Abbot is always slapping Costello around, telling him what to do.

"That's what I'm going to do to you," I whispered when Lisa fell asleep during the movie. "I'm going to take out your braaaaaains."

Whenever Mom goes on one of her trips, Uncle Phil moves into the guesthouse in the back. Uncle Phil is cool. He lets us get away with murder except he hit me once when I told him to get a life. He thinks he's in charge, but he isn't. Pamela is. She's the boss. Pamela's our nanny. She also cooks and cleans. Her brother, Cheetoh, does the gardening. They're from the Philippines. Lisa and me like them a lot. They're super nice, a lot nicer than my parents. Cheetoh calls me Ray Ray and Little Man when everyone else calls me Raymond. Pamela makes great scrambled eggs. They slide down your throat all buttery and sweet. Sometimes Mom cooks but it always sucks. Always always. And she never cleans up afterward, which I don't think is fair, but how am I supposed to tell *her* that? How am I supposed to tell her anything?

When Mom's away things are way more laid back around the house. Pamela still cooks and cleans and all, but

she seems a lot happier about it. Cheetoh and Uncle Phil
hang out by the pool and smoke dope all day. Uncle Phil
says when I turn thirteen I can start smoking, but that's not
for a while.

The best part about Mom being gone is I can take off
on my skateboard with Stevo whenever I want. As long as
I'm back for lunch and dinner, no one asks me where I'm
going, where I've been. Sometimes I hide in the pool shed
to see if they talk about me when I'm not around, but they
never do.

It was a very simple procedure.

I poured Nyquil into Lisa's teacup and made her sip it
until the whole bottle was gone. She drank it like it was
Kool-Aid. I told her to go change into her swimsuit. She
went into her room, and when she didn't come out, I went
in and found her asleep on the bed with her stuffed animals,
a little purple puddle of drool on the bedspread.

I put her in the laundry caddy and wheeled her out to
the garage. It wasn't easy, but I got her into the washing
machine sink. I won't tell you how I got the brains out
because I told Stevo and he got sick on his shoes, and I had
to tell him I was only kidding. All it took was a little crack.
They practically came out by themselves.

Mom is always talking about the islands. The islands
this, the islands that. We were watching *Survivor* one night
and I asked if that's what the islands are like.

"No," she said after a while. "That's exactly what I'm
trying to get away from."

When I was little I used to think she meant Catalina

Island, where we went camping before Lisa was born, just me, Mom and Dad. We drove to Long Beach and took the boat across. I almost got sick but I didn't. We saw flying fish and dolphins. We had a tent near the beach. We could see buffalo walking on the ridge. Me and Dad flew a bright blue kite with a silver streamer. Mom laid out in the sand and watched us. We always talked about going back, but we never did.

On a clear day, you can see Catalina from my mom's bedroom upstairs. The islands Mom goes to are far away, which, I guess, is the point.

The operation was a complete success.

Sort of.

At first I thought Lisa's brains totally messed it up. For a couple of days Bengo just walked around like a person, picking things up with its little paws, holding on to the wall like it might fall over. It growled at me every time I came in the room.

It's way better now. I mean *way* better. It doesn't do that stupid pounce thing anymore. It can hang out or watch TV. It can basically do everything a kid can do, only it never gets hurt. If a ball gets stuck on the roof I can throw Bengo up there and it will fetch the ball and throw it down. Then it will walk to the edge of the gutter and jump off. Sometimes it gets snagged in the bushes, but most of the time it just gets up and brushes itself off like it's no big deal. Sometimes it follows me around the house until I stop what I'm doing and play with it. It puts its hands on its hips like my sister used to do, which is totally freaky but also kind of understandable. I mean, it looks like Bengo and everything, but inside it's my sister.

Lisa? She's sleeping in the toy chest, waiting for her brains back.

One of the games Lisa and me used to play was ragdoll. We'd be watching TV or whatever and she'd say "Ragdoll!" and throw herself on top of me. This meant she had turned into a ragdoll and had gone totally boneless. If I wanted her off me, I had to move her myself because she couldn't move. If I wasn't in the mood I'd push her off and tell her to leave me alone. But sometimes I'd be a good sport and move her back onto her side of the couch. Then she'd yell "Ragdoll!" and jump on me again. Sometimes I just let her stay on top of me until she fell asleep, the breathing in her belly getting slower and slower, her dirty hair hanging over our faces like a net.

Saturday was the best day, the strangest day. When Uncle Phil came into the kitchen his eyes were all scratchy and red.

"I hereby declare this I-don't-give-a-shit day," he said.

"You said it, brother," Cheetoh said and poured himself another bowl of Cap'n Crunch.

After breakfast they all went out by the pool, Pamela, Cheetoh, and Uncle Phil.

"Come hang out with us, Ray Ray," Cheetoh said.

So I did.

Pamela was wearing one of Uncle Phil's beer t-shirts and her bathing suit underneath. Her hair was long and wavy and her eyes flashed. She took off her t-shirt and splashed oil all over her dark skin. I'd never seen her in a bathing suit before. She usually wears jeans and sweat shirts. I thought she was kinda fat, especially compared to mom, who is super skinny, but Pamela wasn't fat. She was something else.

"You're gonna get a sunburn," I said and everyone laughed.

"Don't stare," Uncle Phil said, "it's not polite."

I could tell he was serious because he didn't call me a name.

When she got up and walked to the diving board Cheetoh and Uncle Phil got quiet. Pamela went up in the air and came down, a spray of bright water in the sky, her body a shadowy blur skimming along the pool's black bottom.

She looks the same every time I open the toy box: head down and tilted to the side, her left shoulder slumped against the box, her head full of stuffing. Her skin is pale, pale, pale. Paler than I've ever seen it before. She looks cold so I put a blanket inside the box and some peanut M&Ms—her favorite—for when she wakes up.

Bengo's been acting weird. I catch it doing all kinds of stupid stuff. Yesterday I found it standing in the bath-room sink, staring at itself in the mirror. This morning, while I was looking for my flip-flops out by the pool, I saw Bengo on the diving board, its paws hanging over the edge. "No!" I shouted, and it looked at me. It tensed its legs, like it was going to pounce into the pool. The diving board shuddered. I screamed, "No!" over and over again, and I swear it could hear me, that stupid smile stitched onto its face. Stevo stuck his head over the fence, his face all "What the fuck?" Bengo was slumped over, a crumpled-up shape on the edge of the diving board. A ragdoll.

Pamela wakes me up in my room. Her eyes are red. It looks like she's been crying.

"Where's Lisa?"

"Sleepover," I say.

"With who?" she wants to know. Lisa has lots of friends, I can say "Julie" or "Tammi" or "Trish" and it won't make a difference, so I make one up.

"Misty."

Pamela bites her thumbnail, thinks it over.

"Do you want some eggs?"

"Yes."

"How do you want them?"

"Scrambled."

I need to find Bengo so I can give Lisa her brains back, but I can't find him. I looked in the pantry where Pamela keeps her cleaning supplies. I looked on the bottom shelf behind the bar. I looked in Lisa's pile of stuffed animals, but it isn't there. I looked in the trashcans around the side of the house. I looked behind the table in the living room where it jammed itself one time. I even went up on the roof and scanned the yard, front and back. Nothing. The wind blew in from the ocean and I could see the surfers lining up for the waves. The ocean was shiny and bright like mom's lips when she's going out. I go inside and call her at her hotel but she isn't in. They asked if I wanted to leave a message and I hung up the phone.

Something's up with Pamela. It's 9 o'clock at night and she's still in her bathing suit. Her skin looks super dark, and when she walks by the television she looks like a model or something. She paces back and forth, chewing on a fingernail. Uncle Phil tells her to chill.

"Yeah, chill out," I chime in, and she stops pacing.

"Shouldn't Lisa be home by now?"

I shrug, change the channel.

"It's late. What do you want to eat?"

"Nothing," I say, so we don't eat.

A dream comes to me as I'm falling asleep. I'm a roving eyeball, looking for Lisa in the empty rooms of our empty house. The eye goes outside where the pool is all spooky looking, and the power lines crackle and hum. The eye goes right up to the shed. "Here," it seems to say. "Look here."

I pull on my board shorts and go downstairs. The house is quiet and bone cold. The sliding glass door has been left open. I make my way to the pool shed. I put my hand on the latch and hear the sound of a metal chair-leg scraping against the concrete. My insides turn over, and I think of Lisa, wet and cold in the washing machine sink after I rinsed away all the blood.

It's Uncle Phil and Pamela. Uncle Phil is in the lounge chair and Pamela is on top of Uncle Phil. She has her hair piled up in a stack on her head, and she holds it there with her hands. She's totally naked. Uncle Phil's white feet go from side to side, side to side. He goes "Aaaaahhhhh!" Pamela moans and then the hair comes down.

I look in the tool shed but Bengo's not there. This destroys me.

I'm with Stevo on the strand when it hits me: Bengo's in the toy box. I say it over and over again as I skate home: Toy. Box. Toy. Box. The ache in my belly goes away and everything feels warm and golden. I laugh and push Stevo off his skateboard. He falls in the sand and curses at me. He isn't hurt or anything, but he's still mad. "Don't mess with me," I say, "or I'll knock your brains out."

I didn't mean it. It just slipped right out.

I hear the scream when I'm in the rec room playing video games. Feet pounding all over the house. The glass door slides open and shut, open and shut. Scary monsters pop up on the TV screen, and I kill them all.

Pamela and Cheetoh have a powwow in the dining room while Uncle Phil calls my dad's assistant in Malibu. Pamela cries and cries and cries. Cheetoh comes in, sits next to me on the sofa. He puts his arm around my shoulders, makes me lose another life, and now the game is ruined.

THE HITMAN'S HANDBOOK

Watch your back, the Handbook states, *the field of contract killing is denigrated with treachery and deceit. Your vigilance must be deathless and undying. Trust no one.*

Big Elbow Marconi could go along with that. Unfortunately for him, the Handbook didn't offer any advice for when the used car salesman you're supposed to whack waits in the rental car parking lot at Sky Harbor Airport, stuffs you in the trunk of his late-model Buick LeSabre, and drives you hundreds of miles into the wilderness so he can march you up a steep mountain trail at gunpoint, which was precisely Big Elbow's predicament.

Big Elbow, seldom prone to fits of introspection, wondered how the gunman, Larry Lots, a washed-up, ulcer-ridden skunk who'd been stealing from Miserelli for years, had managed to turn the tables so quickly. Miserelli had opened the contract only yesterday, yet someone had tipped Larry off, told him Big Elbow was coming. Big

Elbow imagined his body left out in the open, vulnerable to the cadaverous whims of the wild. He got to thinking about birds, big black birds dropping ravenous out of the sky. So much for deathless vigilance. So much for undying.

The two men made a lot of noise as they stumbled up the trail, Ponderosa pines everywhere. Big Elbow was baffled by the scenery. What was this place, this alpine hinterland north of Phoenix, south of Vegas? Sometimes the shadows were so deep and cold, the air so brisk and still, his body became numb, dark thoughts on the wing. Then the trail turned a corner in the trees, pointing the two men at the bright sun hanging low in the sky, and the desperation fell away like a tiny hat blown off by a strong wind.

The trail coiled around the lip of a scummy pond. The shallow depression sat in a rocky clearing, fouling the thin air. On the other side of the pond, the trees gave way to a dry meadow choked with grass. No houses, no fences. Just rocky outcroppings and a shitload of scrub. It startled Big Elbow to stumble upon a flat meadow so high in these desert mountains. He stopped in his tracks where the sunlight streamed through the trees. Larry bumped into him and freaked-out, resuming his spastic, two-handed grip on the revolver.

"Miserelli sent you, didn't he?"

Big Elbow sighed. Here's this greaseball, stealing brazenly from his business partner, but he's got to drive halfway across a desert and climb a mountain to hear what everyone from Chicago to San Jose has known for years.

"I wouldn't know anything about that," Big Elbow said, eyes fixed on the other side of the meadow. "What's this all about anyway?"

"Nature hike," Larry said.

Big Elbow, born and raised in Elizabeth, New Jersey, couldn't give a shit about trees if he tried. The wilderness weirded him out, made him nervous. He squatted in the dirt. This was no killer, he reminded himself, this was a car salesman, a thief. He was beginning to feel the first touch of anger, the pointy finger of his temper jabbing at his judgment when Larry surprised him by pressing the cool barrel of the .38 up against the back of his head.

"You didn't answer my question."

Larry "Lots" Lozinsky used his place of employment, a used car lot in North Las Vegas, as a front for his clandestine role as the middleman in a salvage swap scheme. The cars that funneled through the lot were seldom in Larry's care for more than a couple days. Most of the time they came off the carrier from Los Angeles smelling of Pine-Sol and the odor became for Larry the scent of death. It never failed to remind him how these vehicles were obtained.

Larry's end in the scheme was administrative. Safe. Bloodless. Conscionable. He'd ghost the stolen vehicles with titles from automobiles purchased at salvage yards and send them on their way. Money changed hands, but Larry was no killer. Sure, he skimmed an additional percentage before he shipped the money back to Miserelli in Los Angeles—he would have been a fool not to—but the real thieving was left to the predators who jacked the cars. Every once in a while, there would be an account of a particularly messy boost on the evening news. These, for Larry, were the worst of days. He'd crack open a bottle of

Maalox and watch the L.A. broadcasts until he felt sufficiently sick at heart.

Larry knew something was wrong when he was overtaken by a strange feeling at the end-of-quarter sales meeting at the lot on Lake Mead Boulevard. The feeling was accompanied by an uneasy urgency that Larry usually associated with bowel trouble, and it left him shaky and cold, like an icy wave had passed over him and stripped something away in the passing.

He made some phone calls from the Kentucky Fried Chicken joint across the street. All his associates in the scheme were out or unavailable: Joey, Swish, the two Tonys. He couldn't get a hold of anyone. Even his ex-wives were out of reach. Larry wandered into the street and was nearly clipped by a jarhead in a Mini. He hated those cars.

Back at his office, Larry was running out of people to call. When the telephone rang, he snatched it up and was greeted by his repo man, Chester Megs, calling from Los Angeles.

"You step in some shit I ought to know about?"

Larry's mouth went dry. "You know something?"

"I've had a tail on me since Thursday."

"Something's wrong."

"No shit something's wrong."

"What are you doing in Los Angeles?"

"Working."

"Who knew you were coming out?"

"Nobody—shit."

"What? What is it?"

"Don't go nowhere. I'll call you back."

The line went dead. Larry thrummed his fingers on the

desk. He already owed Chester big, not counting the time he'd asked him if he could procure a woman—for one of the Tony's, not for him—and Chester had stared him down through the red nets in his perpetually bloodshot eyes, saying: "I ain't no pimp." Okay, so he wasn't a pimp; he was an overdressed black man with a lot of lady friends. No problem.

The phone rang. Chester again.

"You in big trouble, man. Miserelli sent somebody."

"Sent somebody? What are you talking about?"

"Dude named Marconi. Red-eye. Phoenix. Tomorrow."

Larry didn't know what to say.

"You got any muscle out here?" Chester asked.

"No. Just you."

"That's a big negative. You're gonna have to handle this yourself."

Larry blinked at the light, ran his fingers through his thinning hair. "I need your help."

"It'll cost you."

Chester came out of the house wearing a t-shirt and party hat from his daughter's birthday party that was still going strong. Larry was sitting in the Prelude Chester had asked for—nice body, needed tires—and he told the man to sit tight. Chester let him cool it for an hour before he rapped on the driver's side window, startling the salesman awake. The man looked wiped, like he'd gotten into some bad speed, and Chester damn near sent him home.

Larry rolled down the window, started gibbering nonsense.

"Not here," Chester said.

At his favorite diner on Owens Avenue, Chester slid the shoebox across the table and went to work on his Rueben, best damn sauerkraut in North Las Vegas.

"What is it?" Larry asked.

"A howitzer. What you think?"

Larry lifted a corner of the shoebox, peeked inside, dropped the lid.

"Jesus."

Chester finished his sandwich and tried to remember his father's last words. He'd been laid up a week when he called Chester into his bedroom, bid him to sit close, and offered one last bit of advice. It seemed like those words would be useful to Chester right now, but damned if he could remember what his old man had said. He'd spent the week high on brandy and cocaine, and the details were kind of hazy.

"You can pick up the check and I'll take you to the airport, or I'll pay and you can call a cab. Your choice."

"That's it?" Larry asked. "This is the extent of your help?"

"What do you want, a handbook? You find your man and do him. It ain't complicated."

"But—"

"But nothing. The guy's name is Marconi. His flight information's in the box."

"How will I know him?"

"You feel a chill," Chester said, a piece of sauerkraut stuck in his teeth, "I suggest you look up. You probably standing in his shadow."

*

Big Elbow stared at the dark pool, keeping an eye on Larry's reflection in the scummy water. A faint stirring in the pine needles distracted him. Larry saw it, too. The car salesman turned and trained his gun on something that scurried across the forest floor and disappeared.

"Did you see that?" Big Elbow asked.

"See what?"

"A chipmunk."

"That wasn't chipmunk, it was a squirrel."

"Bullshit."

"Chipmunks ain't got tails like that. What do you know?"

"You think I never seen a squirrel before?"

"Say it!" Larry screamed.

"Say what?"

"Say it was a squirrel."

"You can't make me—"

The bullet zinged between his thighs and nicked him in the balls. He dropped to the ground.

"Say it!" Larry screamed.

"Jesus, Larry. A rat's a rat." Big Elbow rolled over on his back, clutching his crotch.

"Get up," Larry said. "We still got a ways to go."

"You shot me in the nuts. I'm not going anywhere."

"I'm not asking you again."

"Every time you lose your nerve, you come back twice as strong. Just like a car salesman."

"You don't know me..."

"Save it, thief."

"Who are you to call me a thief? You're a murderer! An assassin!"

"I don't think so. An assassination changes the course of history. When a little pimple like you gets popped, nothing changes. Nobody cares."

Larry pointed the weapon at Big Elbow's head. "How dare you!"

Larry's voice was carried away in a gust of wind. The gun wilted in his hand like a flower and his arms sagged at his sides. Big Elbow saw the window of opportunity opening up before him and wasted no time taking advantage of it. He lunged and knocked Larry on his back. The first shot sailed high, up into the trees; the second spun Big Elbow around and flung him to the ground.

He waited—lips parted, his face pressed into the red dirt—for Larry to get up and kick him in the ribs like an old tire. He lay perfectly still. He started to get that awful feeling again he'd had when Larry got the drop on him at the airport. The sun filtered through the trees, laying down ladders of light, dappling the edges of the forest. The brilliance of it hurt his eyes, and the more he tried to shut it out the worse he felt. And what was that sickening smell? Pine-Sol?

Larry stood up but Big Elbow was ready for him. He kicked him in the knee and knocked him down. They struggled, but not for long. Big Elbow grabbed a fistful of Larry's hair, tilted his head back, and unloaded a right that shattered his nose. He dragged Larry over to the pond and straddled him. He got both hands around Larry's throat and pushed his head into the muck. After about thirty seconds, he pulled him out, gave him a chance to redeem himself.

"Talk."

"The money—"

"What money?" Big Elbow snarled, not entirely in control.

Larry spat brackish water. Big Elbow leaned closer, ear to mouth, and listened to the salesman's last pitch, his absolute best and final offer.

I was right, Larry thought, I'm not like this man at all.

When Larry was finished, Big Elbow pressed the salesman's head even deeper into the pond and held him there. The vague outline of the salesman's features floated to the surface. Big Elbow let the ghoul come out and made a game of chasing the gleam in Larry's eyes from one dark corner to the next until the spark died and gave way to his own grim reflection in the surface of the pond as the cheap souvenir of Larry's last words ran wild in Big Elbow's imagination.

He took the corpse by the ankles and dragged it away from the pond. He ripped the dead man's shirt from his body and tore it into strips. He felt at peace with the world and his role in it. Perhaps the wilderness had done him some good after all.

He took off his suit and bandaged his armpit where the bullet had grazed his arm. There was nothing he could do about his ballsack. Donning the dark suit again, Big Elbow unsuccessfully tried to turn away the pain traveling up and down his arm and busied himself with the task of hiding the body. He left the brass casings where they lay.

Big Elbow relieved Larry of his car keys and dragged him into the forest. He stopped in the shadow of a fallen tree some distance from the trail. The ground along the length of the enormous pine was moist with decay. He propped the dead man up against the rotted wood, leaving Larry with a nice view of the meadow. He liked the wilderness so much? Well now he could look at it for as long as he liked, the rest of eternity even.

He made sure Larry's corpse wasn't visible from the trail, picked up the gun, and threw it in the pond. He stirred the mud at the water's edge until he couldn't see any blood.

Tree limbs creaked like old rope under strain. The assembly to murder commenced in the treetops. Big Elbow wondered how long the black birds had been there, what they'd seen. Something about the silence, the stirring of the trees, told him he was going to get away with it. He stayed with Larry until he counted ten, fifteen, twenty crows overhead, shifting their weight from foot to foot, calling out, as if to say, *Go on, we'll take over from here.*

He knew Miserelli would be pleased with his account of the death of Larry Lots: how he looked him in the eyes and told him who was doing this to him. He would choose his words very carefully, pretending to shake the details loose from his memory with care. He'd tell him how the pine cones exploded underfoot when he stepped on them. The strange red earth, the dark trees, the cold sun. He'd finish with the crows descending on the corpse. He decided to leave the part out where Larry got the drop on him. And if there was any truth to Larry's story that a small fortune lay buried at the foot of a scorched piñon on the other side of the meadow, he'd keep that to himself as well.

Back in L.A., Big Elbow gimped around town paying visits to friends in the business, and Chester Megs followed his every move. Big Elbow had come back from Arizona with a lot more money than he'd left with, which could only mean that Larry had tried to bribe his way out of his situation with money he'd skimmed from the scheme, money Chester had been trying to sniff out for years.

The night Big Elbow was supposed to meet with Miserelli, Chester followed the hitman to an Italian restaurant in Hollywood. Judging by the way the big fellow was throwing money around, it was clear the hitman had no intention of sharing his discovery. Chester watched Big Elbow put away the lasagna, guzzle overpriced Chianti.

After the restaurant had emptied, Big Elbow got up and headed for the exit. There was no need to hurry; Chester had already disabled the alternator on Big Elbow's car. The waiter left the heel of the bottle on Chester's table with the check. As Chester filled his glass with the last of the wine, he remembered what his father had told him on his deathbed so very long ago: *Be wary of a dying man's last words, especially when they are a comfort to you.* Chester stood, polished off the wine, and followed Big Elbow to the parking lot. Someone ought to put that one in the handbook.

EASTWOOD

Dan is here. I'm so sick of Dan. About six months ago Dan became a performance artist. It happened on a Halloween night when Dan, Susie and I went to a party in Silverlake. Dan went as a mechanized simulation of an Elvis Presley impersonator. Elvisbot, he called it. Every hour or so he broke into "Suspicious Minds." Dan was a hit.

Susie was a piece of sushi. I went as The Man With No Name. I have to admit, Elvisbot was pretty cool, and Dan never came out of character, not even when I told him how much I was enjoying sleeping with his girlfriend.

Dan is in my living room wearing high-water khaki slacks and a faded pocket t-shirt. He's been wearing the same clothes since high school. His blue eyes burn with an intensity I find exasperating because I know it means he's going to stay until he gets whatever it is he has to tell me off his chest. He's all geeked-up about his latest project. It's pretty much all he talks about these days, and I'm sick of it.

"Dude," he says, "check this out."

Dan dresses like a computer programmer but talks like a surfer. He closes his eyes and proceeds to have a fit. It is a pretend fit, but a fit is a fit. He appears to be slashing his body with a sharp instrument that isn't there. He pretends to scream, but no noise comes out. He looks ridiculous.

"So?"

"I'd call it *Man Standing In The Shallows, Ripping Leeches From His Skin.*"

"That's awesome! I was going for *Man Wakes From Dream Of Cutting Himself With A Kitchen Knife And Finds Band-Aids All Over His Body, Which He Proceeds To Rip Off*, but leeches is way better! I'm going to work on that some more. Thanks, dude!"

"No problem."

Dan leaves. I go to the bedroom and open the closet door. Susie is sitting in the corner eating salted almonds from a can.

"Is he gone?"

"Yeah."

"Is he coming back?"

"I don't think so. He's working on a new project."

Susie thinks this over, munching on an almond. She puts the plastic lid on the can and sticks it on a shelf next to her checkbook. Susie spends a lot of time worrying about her finances, which are nonexistent.

"He might come back," she says. "You know how much your approval means to him."

"I guess."

"I'm going to stay for a while." There's an awkward

silence that feels intentionally inserted. "If you don't mind."

"Of course not," I say at length, because this is a game that two can play. "Do you want to watch a movie later?"

"I don't think so. Will you shut the door on your way out?"

I don't know why Dan annoys me so much lately. Maybe it's because I'll say something like, "You're really starting to annoy me, Dan. Why don't you get the hell out of here?" And he'll come back with, "Did you know Rosebud was William Randolph Hearst's nickname for his girlfriend's vagina?" Or: "Isn't it interesting that *The Trial* was filmed in the train station that later became the Musée d'Orsay?" It's bad enough he doesn't bother to ask me if I give a shit about Orson Welles, he just dumps his useless trivia on me. Worst of all, we both know the Musée d'Orsay is an art museum on the banks of the Seine in the middle of Paris that houses Western art dating from 1848 to 1914, and that neither one of us has a chance in hot hell of ever seeing it.

Then there's this: he stole my laugh. This was back before he became an artist. Maybe it was one of his first projects. I don't know, but I told him to give it back and he acted like he didn't know what I was talking about. So I did what anyone would do. I stole his girlfriend.

Dan pretty much forced her on me. Not in a kinky way or anything, he just lost interest in her as he became absorbed with his projects, and I started sleeping with Susie without thinking about what I was getting into. Now I'm no longer sure who's getting the sour end of the deal.

Susie and I hardly ever have sex anymore, which bothers me more than I let on. Her moods are indecipherable to me. I'd like to ask Dan how to get her out of my closet, but I'm pretty sure he wouldn't have a clue.

Halfway through *For A Few Dollars More*, Dan comes over. I hit pause, hoping he'll get the picture and keep it quick, but Dan never gets the picture.

"Dude, I've refined *Man In The Shallows*. Want to see it?"

I don't answer. I know he'll show me anyway. Dan has another pseudo-fit, which I find sad and depressing. Dan's not a bad person. He doesn't deceive people or hurt anyone, but his earnestness makes him an easy target, and for some reason I always seem to be the one looking down the barrel, putting him in the crosshairs.

"Why aren't you saying anything?"

"I'm doing my own project," I say. "It's called *Inscrutable Cynic Cherishes Silence*."

"That's not funny."

"It's not supposed to be. It's a zen thing."

"Zen from a guy who watches spaghetti westerns? I'd say you're conflicted."

I don't answer this. I just stare at the frozen screen. Clint Eastwood in an Italian flick financed by Germans, riding an Arab horse across a Spanish desert, pretending it's the American West. This makes sense to me; Dan does not.

He slams the door on his way out. I sense Susie standing in the doorway behind me.

"Why do you hate him?" she asks.

Big sigh.

"I don't hate him," I answer. "What makes you think that?" But Susie's not behind me anymore. She's retreated to the cloister of my closet.

My phone rings.

"Mr. Fontainebleau?"

I should explain that my name is not Fontainebleau. Fontainebleau is Dan's name for me. He gave it to me after we watched a caper flick set in Miami. All the bad guys stayed at the Hotel Fontainebleau. He said that was a good name for me: a safe house for evildoers. Hearing a stranger use it tells me something terrible has happened.

"Yes, what is it?"

"There's been an accident," the voice says.

Dan has my number programmed into his cell phone. It says "A. Fontainebleau." I never asked what the "A" stood for, but now I'd like to know. I'm the only person he ever calls, the only number stored in his phone. He'd call Susie, I suppose, but Susie's never home.

"What kind of an accident?"

"A car accident."

"How is he?"

"He's laughing, but it's not appropriate to his situation."

"Is he going to make it?" I ask, but the voice on the other end of the line won't tell me. He gives me the address instead. It's only a block away. I thank the man and end the call.

I go to the closet and tell Susie the news. She looks up at me and blinks a few times. Susie doesn't wear much make-up and although she's not as hot as she used to be I understand that her appearance is a direct reflection of the choices she has made, good and bad but mostly bad, and this has something to do with me. Right now she looks confused.

"Are you coming?"

"Oh," she says, "you mean now?"

Dan is laid out on the sidewalk. He looks pretty bad, but I can't help but wonder if this is another one of his projects. There is a jacket wadded up under his head. I was with him when he bought it at the thrift store but now it's soaked with blood. Dan's breathing is uneven. It comes in sharp gasps, like an espresso machine. His cheeks are flecked with foam.

"Ambulance is on the way," the man with Dan's phone says.

"Jesus."

"Tell me about it."

Susie and I kneel at Dan's side. Susie takes one hand. I take the other. Dan smiles, happy to see us.

"What's going on here?" I ask.

"*Rabid Mime Mowed Down by Motorcar.*"

"Dan, this is no time for jokes."

"Elvisbot has left the building." The smile on his face gets bigger and bigger.

I wipe his mouth with the cuff of my shirtsleeve. Susie starts to cry.

"Look." Dan lifts up his t-shirt. He's taped a piece of string to his stomach. At the end of the string is a metal ring.

"Pull it."

"Dan—"

"No, it's okay. Pull it."

Susie nods, but there's no way she's going to pull the string. I have to do it.

I hook my finger around the ring. It is warm to the touch, like a coin held too long in the hand.

"Are you ready?"

Dan nods like he never thought I'd ask. I pull the string and he laughs my laugh. Perfect and mechanical. I get it: he's giving me my laughter back. His smile is bigger than ever. Susie throws her arms around Dan's thin shoulders and heaves huge silent sobs.

Dan's hands flutter to his stomach and become still.

I pull the ring again, but nothing happens. My best friend is broken.

BIG LONESOME

CARSON CITY BREAKOUT

On a Sunday morning in the middle of September, the Cinema gang blew a hole in the wall at the Nevada State Penitentiary, facilitating the escape of eleven last-chancers and one badly stunned boy.

Billy Cinema, the famous stagecoach robber, authored the plot. The bank sneak, Jubal McDowd, and a forger named Lefty Burwell, lent their assistance. Each had passed word of the breakout to associates in the penitentiary. The convicts gathered at the eastern end of the yard at the appointed hour. Those who'd never worked with dynamite dawdled near the wall and were denied the chance to repeat the blunder.

The explosion sounded like a preacher's promise of Judgment Day, and was heard throughout Carson City. Barbers froze mid-snip. Bankers paused and lost count. Even the dancers at the nearby saloon sensed something was amiss even though the player piano hadn't missed a beat. When the smoke cleared, there was more hole than wall, and the convicts hooted and hollered as they made their escape.

Young Michael Conklin had never heard of Billy Cinema. He'd had the misfortune of stealing a chicken from a coop that had lost a bird a week for six weeks straight, and the lawman who placed Michael under arrest told him they were charging him for the whole lot.

Michael had got down on his knees and begged the Good Lord to intervene. Even though he knew it was blasphemy to attribute the mischief of man to the Creator's plan, he felt that his prayers had been answered, for if the prison wall had not been divinely smote, then Michael didn't know what smote was.

"What are you waiting for?" Blink, an old one-eyed codger whose passion for window smashing made him a frequent guest, shouted over the din. "The warden just granted you a pardon!"

Blink may have only had one eye, but he had a way of fixing it on a person that was awfully convincing, and Michael followed his cellmate through the roiling cloud of dust to freedom.

The stables at the nearby Vanderpool Hotel supplied the convicts with horses. Blink seized a good strong mare and mounted her. Michael stood off to the side.

"Can't you ride?"

"Never learned how."

"Where you from, boy?"

"San Francisco."

Blink sighed. "Get on."

Michael climbed onto the horse. Blink turned the beast around, but Jubal blocked their path. There was blood on his forehead, but he didn't appear wounded. He had chain bracelets inked on both wrists and his green eyes glared at Michael.

"What's your name?"

"Simon Tucker, but folks call me Blink."

"I ain't talking to you. Who's the boy?"

"A chicken rustler."

Michael winced at the description.

"Can he talk?"

"I can talk," Michael said as defiantly as he knew how.

"You coming with us?"

"Yessir."

"If you light out, I'll put a bullet in your back. Understand?"

"Yessir."

Jubal presented Blink with a six-shooter and spurred his horse east toward the river. Blink gave out a rebel yell and made a big show of waving the six-shooter around as they galloped down the street and shot out all the windows of the feed store. Michael figured Blink was a harmless old coot, but when a man outside the post office reached inside his topcoat, Blink put a bullet in his neck, and Michael figured he'd figured wrong.

THE GERMAN

The bounty hunter stood at the trailhead and surveyed the expanse of desert before him. Nothing but crusty scrubland as far as he could see. To the west: a salty sink crawling with snakes and scorpions; to the east: a wasted plain stippled with sun-bleached bones. It was hotter than donkey piss and as dry as beans. He had a far piece to go and this was the way to get there.

He reached into his saddlebag, broke off a marble-sized piece of rock salt, and pushed it around his mouth with his tongue. It was a trick he'd learned from an old prospector who'd lived forty years in the desert and died in his nightshirt at a Yerba Buena brothel.

The bounty hunter flicked the reins and slowly picked his way across the blighted plain, skirting the old dead lake. By the time he'd sucked the salt nugget down to the size of a baby's tooth, the sun was a puddle that stained the clouds pink and purple. He tied the horse to a piñon and lay his bedroll down in the scrub. He took off his boots and drifted off with his six-shooter tucked in the crook of his elbow. He hadn't thought of a name for the horse yet, but one would come.

MICHAEL CONKLIN'S LIFE OF CRIME

Michael Conklin spent the first ten years of his life in a whorehouse. His father was a Peruvian sailor; his mother a Montgomery Street whore. When the brothel burned to the ground, his mother hit the streets and was dead by the end of the week, stabbed in an argument over the price of her company. Michael witnessed the murder.

He was hiding in the alley behind a Chinese boarding house. The stench of rotting noodles rose from the slop at his feet as he sized up the mark. The women at the brothel had taught him two things: how to charm the fairer sex, and how to recognize drunkenness in men. The man his mother was engaged with, a filthy hardscrabble mountaineer, was ripe for plucking.

Michael heard them bickering and made his move just as the mountaineer punched a knife into his mother's belly. Michael slashed the man across the back of his knees. He collapsed facedown in the sewer and flopped about like an eel. Michael straddled the mountaineer, jerked his head back, and cut his throat.

He went to his mother, who'd propped herself up under a boarded-up kitchen window, and knelt by her side. She seemed strangely calm, as if she'd been preparing for this moment all her life.

"Take his money."

"I won't leave you."

"Don't be a fool."

Michael sifted through the dead man's pockets and found a leather satchel plump with coins. He cut it loose and stuffed it down his pants as a large man in a black cassock grabbed him by the collar and dragged him down the alley. Michael called out to his dying mother, tried to resist, but the man threw him into the street where a gaggle of citizens had gathered to see what the commotion was all about. Thus it came to pass that Michael Conklin entered the alley a boy and came out a killer.

THE DISPOSITION

The Cinema gang put their boss on a stagecoach and spirited him away to St. Louis. He was gunned down in a raid outside a faro house he was fond of frequenting. His last words testified to the fact that he liked his chances in the afterlife just fine.

The desperadoes split up at the Carson River. Jubal went down river; Lefty went up, leading his men into the teeth of the posse that had been dispatched from Dayton. They retreated south, but they pushed their horses too hard, and they were massacred at the Mexican Dam.

Jubal's crew fared better. Although he'd been incarcerated for a murder he'd committed in Virginia City, Nevada, Jubal was California born and bred, and his knowledge of the borderlands served the desperadoes well. He led them east through the Pine Nut Mountains and they traveled all that day and long into the night.

Michael had never been so exhausted. He dozed off as the surefooted horses sent rocks skittering down the escarpments. He kept waking up just as he was about to slide out of the saddle and plunge headfirst into the shale.

The desperadoes watered the horses and rested at a hidden spring high up in the mountains. They changed riders to keep the horses fresh and set out again at dawn. They crossed Smith Valley and reached Hot Springs shortly after midnight. Michael figured the longer he stayed with Jubal, the better his chances of sharing his fate. Michael didn't want to dance at the end of a rope or get gunned down in some barren meadow, and started to plot his escape. His plan was simple: sleep during the day to conserve his strength and make his move at night while the others slept. That morning, shortly before dawn, he lay by Blink's side, memorizing the pattern of his breathing. When he spied a glimmering in the pocket of the old man's skull, Michael told himself his eyes were playing tricks on him. He was never so grateful to see the sun.

The convicts pushed south toward Sulfur Springs. Michael's throat hurt, his head ached, and his ass was mighty sore. Worst of all was Blink's stink, which caused Michael to return over and over again to the open sewer behind the Chinese boarding house.

They reached Elbow Joe's in the small hours of the morning, slept until sun-up, cooked a pair of rabbits Jubal had shot, and pressed on. Later, Michael woke to the sound of an argument. Some of the men wanted to know why they were heading east when California lay to the west. Jubal advised the loudest of the lot to keep the hole in his face shut or he'd give him another one, and that settled the matter.

A few hours later, Jubal dismounted and led his horse to a stand of cottonwoods. Blink did the same and before long all the men were huddled at the edge of a stream, splashing water on their faces and drinking from their dirty hands. Blink squatted by Jubal's side and dipped his hat in the water.

"How far back you reckon they are?"

"Who?"

"The posse."

"A hundred miles."

"But that would put them back in Carson City," Blink said, making his confusion plain.

"That's right."

"How do you figure?"

"Ever been in a posse?"

"No."

"Well I have. They set out hot for blood and hollering for justice, but once they get on the trail their tempers cool, and they start missing their beds."

"How long have we been in California?" Michael asked.

If the boy's question surprised Jubal, he didn't show it.

"You know this country, boy?"

"No, sir. Don't care for California."

"You'd rather we left you back in Carson City?"

"No, sir. Don't care for Nevada none neither."

"How old are you?"

"Fourteen."

Jubal laughed, whacked his dusty hat against his knee, and slipped it back on his head.

"Reckon all that sleep you been skipping done slowed your bones from growing."

SONOMA SHAKEDOWN

Michael had given the Irish priests at the orphanage his mother's name, but he had no information about the day or year of his birth. One thing the orphanage had in common with the brothel was that birthdays were neither celebrated nor acknowledged. Even though Michael was big and strong enough to pass for someone considerably older, he had a baby face that gave him away. It didn't matter to Michael if he was ten or twelve or fourteen years old when every day of his hateful existence at the orphanage seemed to last a lifetime.

Each boy worked all day and brought his wages to the priests if he expected a hot supper and a berth in the dormitory. Father Oliver, the man who'd rescued Michael from the sins of San Francisco, supplied the orphan with the brushes and tins of polish he needed to earn his keep as a bootblack. It took Michael a while to understand he was the envy of the others because he didn't have to rent his equipment.

"What are you," they taunted him, "some Mexican bastard?"

"I'm Michael Conklin and I'll thrash the whole lot of you!"

No one took the challenge. Michael was prepared to fight to the last because he, unlike them, had something to lose, something to live for, and they knew it the way they knew not to touch a hot kettle or go running across thin ice.

Michael had a keen memory and a knack for numbers, and it wasn't long before his customers had him delivering messages around Sonoma. Father Oliver was so pleased with this development that he moved Michael out of the boys' dormitory and installed him in a storage room off the rectory. He even gave him his own cot.

Every night, Michael pored over the contents of the mountaineer's satchel. Buried in a sheaf of crude letters from a cousin in Wisconsin was the deed to a mine in a place called Big Lonesome. The letters testified to the mountaineer's belief that the mine was loaded with gold but would require an enormous amount of "kapitul and laburr" to extract it. A splendid map indicated Big Lonesome's location at the edge of the Eastern Sierras. Michael imagined claiming the mine and naming it after his mother. He studied the map until he'd memorized every line, and the name of the town and the feeling in his heart were one and the same.

One night, Father Oliver invited Michael up to his room for bible study. After several glasses of port he accosted Michael in a friendly, but altogether un-Christian-like manner. Michael went along for a while and then knocked the priest out with a blow from the wine bottle. He relieved the priest of his legal tender, quit the orphanage, and lit out for the Sierras.

The money might have lasted for months in a place like Sonoma, but in the mountain towns and mining camps accommodations were scarce and prices dear. Sometimes Michael paid nothing at all simply by knocking on the door of the local whorehouse and asking if anyone had seen his mother, which never failed to stir the sympathies of the women of the establishment, many of whom had wayward bastards of their own. Wherever Michael went the women doted over him, and this had a way of turning the men against the youngster.

"When was it you said you was moving along?" the proprietor would inevitably ask.

"Tomorrow."

"That's what I figured."

"Tomorrow's my birthday."

The man would mumble his congratulations and lie about some pressing matter, and the next day his wife would see him off with a meal and something extra for the road. If he had one birthday, he had twenty, but by the time he reached Carson City he was flat busted, and no one gave a damn how old he wasn't.

THE GOOD WITCH OF BIG LONESOME

Misty Meadows had been cleaning the chalkboard at

the schoolhouse when a swirling dizziness came over her. All the light bled out every bright thing in the room and the dark was infused with a liquid intensity. Then the visions came: a riderless horse, a silk scarf soaked with blood, a savage with yellow eyes. The light traded places with the dark and she stood trembling against the chalkboard until she could compose herself. She excused the children from their lessons and sent everyone home. Several hours later, Henry Mechalar noticed the schoolhouse door had been left open and found Misty seated at her desk, staring at the cold stove in the corner with chalk dust in her hair, her face whiter than a puddle of milk.

As was her habit, Misty told no one of her visions. It wouldn't do for the township's only schoolteacher and the wife of sheriff's deputy Abner Meadows to go around claiming she saw ghostly glimpses of things that couldn't be explained. So she kept them to herself—most of the time. When Edgar Dawson was found dead in his cabin, Misty's gentle prodding directed her husband to the heap of rusty saw blades at the mill where Abraham Minton's blood-spattered hatchet was found. Or when Mortimer Harley expired in his soup, it was Misty who encouraged Abner to pay a visit to the apothecary in Aurora where the widow Harley's sister worked on weekends. Misty's husband didn't know about her visions and she often wondered if the knowledge would stop him from seeking comfort in the arms of other women, namely Boticelli Moon, the Celestial proprietress of the Gentlemen's Bath House and Shoe Shoddery, a woman whose name hadn't been associated with virtue since before the Gold Rush.

Misty walked to the town square to learn what she

171

could about the visions. Tom Sweeney had rolled his wagon up to the barbershop and was doing brisk business in corn spirits. The men of the town strutted about with their weapons while the women stood in groups, shaking their heads. Misty saw Henry's sister, Dot Mechalar, standing with Maggie Cassidy and Elizabeth Kertz, and stopped to talk.

"What's all this fuss about?"

"The posse from Bishop turned back at Independence," Dot answered.

"Now it's up to them," Maggie added, indicating the men in the square.

"*They're* going after the convicts?" Misty asked.

The women nodded as one. Misty considered the news and looked up in time to see her husband come thundering into the square atop his horse, Solstice. A shout went up as the men hurrahed and shook their rifles. Abner was freshly shaved and his cheeks were flushed. He slipped from the saddle, removed a scarf that Misty was certain she had never seen before and stuffed it into his saddlebag.

"Are you unwell, Misty?" Dot asked.

"You look a fright," Maggie agreed.

Misty squawked something unintelligible and fainted dead away.

DOCTOR KLAUSEN'S WORKSHOP

High up in the mountains, one of Jubal's men stumbled upon a trapper's cabin. They ransacked the place and found a cache of smoked meat and unadulterated whiskey stowed beneath the floorboards. The half-starved convicts guzzled their allotments and abandoned their wits.

Whenever it was Michael's turn to drink, he let the nasty stuff dribble down his chin. Still, after several rounds of this his head felt empty and his belly burned.

The liquor loosened the desperadoes' tongues and heated their tempers, and for the first time since joining the convicts, Michael was afraid.

After they'd drunk all the whiskey, Jubal threw a horse blanket around his shoulders and told everyone to go to bed. The louder they grumbled the faster they fell asleep, and soon even Jubal was snoring.

Michael slipped out of the cabin and ran down the dark mountain as fast as he dared. He had no horse, no food, no weapons, and no clear notion of his whereabouts.

After a few hours of hard travel, he curled up in the hollow of a felled tree and slept for a spell. Strips of bacon sizzling in butter bedeviled his dreams and he woke up swearing he could smell coal burning somewhere close.

Crazed with hunger, Michael sought the source of the smell. After a few minutes of walking he felt something clutch his ankles and was hoisted into the air. A buck-skinned Chinaman came at him with a Bowie knife. Michael struggled to free himself from the trap, but it was no use. He was caught. Michael shut his eyes and got the wind knocked out of him when he hit the ground. He opened his eyes and saw the Chinaman wasn't alone. Emerging from the trees was a half-naked fellow with skin the color of tree-bark. His head was encased in a cylinder shaped like a cereal tin with big yellow eyes and a crooked smile that looked to Michael like they'd been painted on.

The Chinaman cut Michael loose, sheathed his knife and motioned for him to follow him into the woods.

Michael obliged and the strange man fell in behind him as they made their way down a path in the forest. They came to a heavily rutted road that took them to a clearing where a soot-blackened warehouse billowed smoke. It was the sort of place Michael expected to see in a San Francisco shipyard, not at the base of the mountains in the wilds of California.

Upon entering the workshop Michael felt as if he had been transported to a strange new world. An enormous hole had been dug in the center of the shop, and a network of catwalks crisscrossed the upper dimensions so that the place felt much larger than it looked from the outside. All manner of machinery made a terrific racket: whizzing and whirring from above, grunting and groaning below. A tremendous clanking was general throughout the work-shop, like a crate of railroad spikes rattling around a copper kettle, particularly in the hole where the digging never seemed to stop.

Michael wandered over to the edge and looked down. Sulfur, steam, and ammoniac fumes wafted up. He could see the mouths of many tunnels. Machines hammered at the earth and sifted through the soil. Some machines seemed to have no purpose other than to grapple with other machines in ways that Michael didn't understand.

The Chinaman disappeared but the weird-looking man stayed with Michael. He was even stranger looking in the light. Wherever Michael went, the man followed.

"What do you want?"

The man just stood there with that clumsy smile paint-ed onto his pail-shaped head.

"Who are you?"

"'What are you?' would be a better question," a voice boomed from above. Michael looked up and saw a man dressed in an oil-spattered smock peering over the edge of the catwalk.

"Hello," he said, smiling broadly. "I'm Doctor Klausen. You've already met my assistant, Wing, and this splendid specimen is Tonka. Who might you be?"

"I'm Michael Conklin."

"Please make yourself at home, Michael. Is there anything I can do for you?"

"Tell Tonka to get away from me."

"I'm afraid I can't do that."

"Why not?"

"I've asked Tonka to stop you from leaving."

"You can't keep me here."

"If you mean 'can't' in that I lack the legal authority to deprive you of your liberty, you are correct; but if by 'can't' you mean I am incapable of keeping you, a fugitive from justice, here against your will, you are mistaken. Hungry?"

Michael nodded.

"Good. We'll talk more once you've recovered from your ordeal."

Wing appeared at Michael's elbow with a bowl of steaming soup. Michael figured his hunger and exhaustion were making him delirious and he'd crossed over into a place that was allergic to reason; but soup was soup and he accepted the offer. Michael sat down and ate, and was dreaming of sailing up the Sacramento River aboard an ironclad ship well before the soup turned cold.

SHOOTOUT AT MIRROR LAKE

Misty didn't recover in time to say goodbye to Abner, and even if she had, her nurses wouldn't have let her see him off. She was as beloved by the women in the town as her husband was by the men, and Abner's infidelities, which were as numerous as they were indiscrete, made the women fiercely protective of their schoolteacher.

Just as Abner and his men were setting out, a lucky boon befell them. Digger Morton, the old trapper who kept a place near Mirror Lake in the shadow of Wotan's Throne, informed him that the fugitives from Carson City had spent the night in his cabin. Abner let out a yell and spurred his men into the mountains.

Misty left her sickbed to a chorus of protests, but she did not abide their arguments. Her decision had nothing to do with Abner or the others. She had lessons to plan, copybooks to grade, and her chalkboard still needed a proper cleaning.

The women of Big Lonesome spent a leisurely evening together, enjoying the novelty of one another's company. Then, just as Misty had foreseen, Solstice returned. Misty was outside the schoolhouse stacking the firewood she'd just finished splitting when Solstice came trotting along—riderless and alone. Misty whistled for her and Solstice heeded her master's wife's command. A silk scarf, slick with blood, was knotted around the pommel of Abner's saddle. Misty didn't need her second sight or Digger Morton's report from Mirror Lake to know the Carson City convicts had made Misty a widow.

FAMILY REUNION

Over a breakfast of salt beef, hard rolls, and apricot preserves, Doctor Klausen explained to Michael that he'd been an engineer by trade and a sailor by profession, and had combined the two skills by enlisting in the Confederate Navy and helping William P. Williamson's men overhaul the *Merrimack*'s engines, which the Union had seen fit to leave scuttled in the mud of the Elizabeth River in his native Virginia. Michael in turn explained how he'd found himself a willing hostage of the most wanted men in the West. The doctor proved to be a sympathetic listener.

"How old are you?"

"Fourteen."

"You're not a day older than twelve."

"I am so. Today's my birthday."

"What day is it?"

"___"

"You don't know, do you?"

"No, sir."

"I have some good news and some bad news. Which would you like to hear first?"

"The bad news."

"Your companions have just wiped out the posse from Big Lonesome."

The name set off a little explosion in Michael's head and he thought for the hundredth time that week of the deed he'd had the foresight to sew into the sole of the boot on his left foot.

"What's the good news?"

"You have an uncle."

177

"I do? Who?"

"Me."

Michael's rising anger helped him hide his disappointment.

"I don't understand."

"We're going into town," the doctor elaborated. "I'm going to introduce you as my nephew."

"Why would you do that?"

"Big Lonesome needs our help."

Michael nodded, tapping his left foot to the clank and clamor of Doctor Klausen's digging machines.

THE THIRD "R"

The bounty hunter sat in a Bishop saloon, struggling over a bit of 'rithmatic. He'd been told eleven men escaped the state penitentiary. Six had been slaughtered at the Mexican Dam and the rest had ridden south to California. The last time he'd checked, eleven minus six meant five, but here was this fellow by the name of Scobie Lawrence telling him he'd seen six men watering four horses at the Owens River south of Independence not more than a week ago.

"Are you certain?"

"Five men and a boy. A Mexican by the smell of it."

This bothered the bounty hunter enough to ride back to Independence and telegraph the warden in Carson City. No sense in looking for a body, he thought, if folks don't know it's missing.

A MECHANICAL PROPOSAL

If Digger had seen the wagon coming he might have

put that foolish banjo of his down, but he hadn't seen it, and he kept plucking away until the wagon was practically at the foot of the courthouse stairs. Misty was on her way back from delivering books and stopped to see what was afoot.

Two men rode up front—a lanky gentleman and dark-haired boy. The former consulted his timepiece and stood to address the townsfolk crowding into the square. Misty moved closer for a better look.

"People of Big Lonesome," the gentleman began, "your hour of darkness has passed. A brighter day is nigh."

Digger Morton, whose foul-smelling buckskins now featured a sheriff's star, pushed his way to the front.

"State your business!"

"I have come to remove the stain that blights this fair town!"

"Speak plainly or clear out."

"The convicts responsible for killing your men have taken refuge in the mountains. Winter is coming. It won't be long before they visit more bloodshed upon your town."

Angry murmurs circulated throughout the square.

"My name is Doctor Klausen and I have a proposal. With the assistance of my nephew here, I will bring these foul fellows to justice."

Misty had heard enough.

"We need protection, not another foolish crusade," she said.

The doctor smiled. "I assure you, no innocent man, woman, or child will come to harm."

"How can you guarantee such a thing?"

"I have no intention of sending men into the mountains."

"Then whom will you send?"

"My *posse automatos*."

"Your posse auto-what's-it?" Digger asked.

Doctor Klausen whistled and the strangest looking man Misty had ever seen exited the back of the wagon. He was burdened with a boxlike helmet, yet wore only a loincloth, and the mid-day sun made his musculature shine like a thing from another world.

"Who the hell is that?" Digger asked.

"This is Tonka, my very own creation. If you will permit me a demonstration..."

Digger shot an uncertain glance in Misty's direction. She cleared her throat and struggled to get the words out. "I have no objections."

The doctor clapped his hands. Tonka sprang into the air, leaping forward while tumbling backward, and landed on his feet. Misty gasped along with the rest of the crowd. Something under her ribs came loose, like the hot core of a fire engulfing the fuel it will consume.

Tonka circled the wagon and, much to Misty's astonishment, lifted it off the ground.

"Ladies and gentlemen," the doctor continued, "Tonka is fast, strong, and utterly without fear. Give me three days, and I will eliminate your desperado problem."

Boticelli Moon, the harlot, pushed her way to the front of the crowd in a ridiculous dress that exposed a fair portion of her oft-handled charms. "What," she asked, "do you require in return for your services?"

The doctor could no longer contain his smile. "Mineral rights," he said with a wink.

THE CARSON CITY SIX

A rider was sent to summon Thaddeus Jackson, a Mormon lawyer from Independence, to draw up the necessary paperwork. Michael accompanied Doctor Klausen back to the workshop to prepare for the siege. The plan to capture the men who the wanted posters were calling "The Carson City Six" seemed straightforward enough: surround the cabin and take the fugitives by surprise. The posters troubled young Michael Conklin; suddenly his hard-won freedom didn't feel much like freedom anymore.

"I want to fight."

"Out of the question." The doctor put his hand on Michael's shoulder. "I need you in town to keep the locals calm. Besides, how would it look if I were to send my very own nephew against hardened criminals?"

"I can take care of myself."

"This is a job for Tonka. It's the job he was made for. Wing and his compatriots will accompany him. I assure you they are quite capable."

Back at the workshop, Doctor Klausen disappeared into one of the tunnels that spread out in every direction from the center of the pit like spokes on a wagon wheel. Michael tried to rest, but the heat and the noise made it difficult to sleep. Whenever he managed to drift off for a few moments, he dreamt of accidents caused by terrible machines. He'd wake with a start and find Tonka watching over him. Tonka seemed less strange now. Michael supposed he was getting used to him. The more he watched Tonka the less machinelike he seemed. Michael had seen him shoo a fly and scratch his leg and these things had a bewildering effect on Michael's imagination. Whoever

181

heard of a machine getting an itch?

Maybe Tonka was more than a machine.

Maybe Tonka wasn't a machine at all.

Maybe he was just some poor Indian the doctor had duped into going around with a bucket on his head.

THE EVIL THAT MACHINES DO

The night before Tonka put Jubal McDowd's criminal career to an end, the doctor took Michael to Boticelli Moon's Gentlemen's Bath House and Shoe Shoddery. In his lavishly appointed suite, the doctor opened a bottle of wine and they toasted their success.

"To victory."

Michael drank his wine and forced a smile. He never felt farther from home.

Doctor Klausen returned to his workshop the next day and Michael spent the morning fielding questions about the operation. Most of the inquiries concerned Tonka.

"Does he eat?"

"What is he made out of?"

"How fast does he go?"

"How long can he go without stopping?"

Michael didn't know the answers to these questions, but he understood their curiosity all too well. Their desire to know was a substitute for another kind of longing. Tonka was sturdy and capable, the most reliable and self-sufficient of all Doctor Klausen's contraptions, although "contraption" struck him as a bit uncharitable. Tonka wasn't so much a thing, but a presence that, Michael realized with a pang, he greatly missed.

Boticelli summoned Michael to her bedchamber. The

velvet curtains were drawn. Candles blazed. Ms. Moon was dressed in her finest delicates, but her perfume reminded Michael of his mother. He confessed everything from his involvement with the Carson City Six to his suspicions regarding Doctor Klausen's designs on the town. He even produced the deed to the Big Lonesome mine, which Ms. Moon surveyed with great interest.

"Where did you get this?"

"From the man who murdered my mother."

Ms. Moon had heard enough. She locked the deed up in the safe just as Digger Morton burst into the parlor.

"The machines have raided Big Lonesome!" he shouted. They've kidnapped Miss Meadows!"

AMBUSH

Blink awoke to find a naked man with a pot on his head standing over him with a knife. Blink lived just long enough to snatch a glimpse of the man's privates.

"Dang," he moaned, the word escaping through a vent that God never intended.

WHEN LOVE COMES,
THE ONLY SIN IS TO RESIST IT

Misty finished reading the last verse of *The Love Song of Hiawatha* and closed the book. Even though he couldn't talk, Misty knew Tonka loved Longfellow. She tried to puzzle some meaning out of the crooked smile that played across his face, but he just sat and stared at the fire he'd built in the cave they inhabited.

Three years of marriage to Abner had not prepared her for Tonka. He was more of a man than the manliest of men.

He possessed incredible focus and was beautiful to watch. No task was too difficult for him. Obstacles dissolved before his will. On the night Tonka came for her, she was paralyzed with a mixture of fear and exhilaration that she found much to her liking. She practically leapt into his arms as he galloped past.

He gave off so much heat she seldom wore clothes in his presence. Modesty was wasted on him. Free of cinches and straps, she found an ease she hadn't known since childhood and discovered a purity of thought without even realizing she'd been searching for it. The irony was not lost on her: she'd had to be captured to find freedom.

Tonka was a reluctant master. He demanded nothing of her. She was the one who initiated the search to determine what was underneath his loincloth. She roused him to passion. The only time she knew discomfort was when he was gone. His frequent absences filled her with fear. What did he do out there in the woods? Hunt? Fish? Lay down with other women? On those nights she'd wrap herself in an old army blanket and pace the cave like a wild animal.

Firelight painted flickering shadows on Tonka's body. She grabbed him by the shoulders and turned him to her. She explored his smooth limbs as if he were a tree she sought to climb, but a swirling vision of the doctor's dark-haired nephew, a bone-white bough, and a noose came over Misty that left her breathless in Tonka's arms.

WHAT WENT WRONG

"Let's start at the beginning, shall we?"

Thaddeus Jackson fingered his mustache as he regarded the man of science who sat in the juror's box. The bench was empty; the gallery was packed. Although everyone present had been reminded several times that the doctor was not on trial, Thaddeus Jackson's demeanor lent the proceedings the air of a tribunal. Michael sat in the gallery next to Ms. Moon.

"How many machines," Thaddeus continued, "did you unleash in the vicinity of Big Lonesome?"

"One," the doctor answered.

"Only one?"

"Yes."

"Are you referring to the machine that goes by the name of 'Tonka'?"

"I am."

"Describe this machine."

The doctor paused and cleared his throat. The women in the gallery fanned themselves into a minor frenzy. Beads of perspiration trickled down their perfumed necks in anticipation of the doctor's reply.

"I modeled Tonka after an Indian."

This revelation produced a murmur in the gallery.

"Are you telling me that you have unleashed a savage in our mountains?"

"Yes, I suppose I am."

"And he's beyond your control?"

"I'm afraid so."

Thaddeus struck the banister of the juror's box with his clenched fist.

"If there is a difference between that which leaps from the witch's cauldron at midnight and is dispatched from your workshop by the light of day, I don't see it!"

"He's only a machine."

"A machine is a reaper! A machine is a printing press! Your creations are abominations before God!"

"What is that on your waistcoat?" the doctor asked.

The lawyer ran his stubby fingers over his stomach until they caught his watch fob and hauled the timepiece out of his pocket. "It's a pocket watch."

"Of course it is. And if you were to take it apart, what would you find?"

The lawyer stared at his watch as if he hoped it would reveal its mysteries to him.

"I'll tell you what you'd find," the doctor continued. "You'd find a machine. Now are you telling me your inability to understand how your watch works causes you to mistrust the information it provides you? Or, following your logic, that when your watch tells you it's time for dinner it's doing the devil's work?"

"Doctor Klausen," Jackson drawled, "your words are as clever as your creations. What you seem to forget is that my pocket watch is not responsible for terrorizing the townspeople of Big Lonesome and running off with the late Abner Meadows' widow!"

Applause erupted from the gallery. Thaddeus withdrew the deed to the Big Lonesome mine and held it up before the gallery.

"Furthermore, I have reason to believe that it was your intention to swindle Big Lonesome out of considerable riches by unlawfully abrogating the mines that rightfully belong to the boy you coerced into posing as your nephew."

The look on Doctor Klausen's face almost made all the trials and tribulations Michael had endured worth it, but then the courthouse doors flew open and a haggard-looking bounty hunter strode into the courthouse with a six-shooter at the ready.

"That boy is a fugitive from the Nevada State Penitentiary and a killer, and I aim to see he hangs for it."

Michael cursed under his breath. First Jubal, then Klausen, now this. Out of the skillet, into the bigger skillet. Maybe he was born unlucky. Maybe he was destined to dangle. Whatever it was, his liberty was once again in jeopardy, only this time it was permanent-like.

ROPE JUSTICE

Michael Conklin was in a fix. When the citizens of Big Lonesome learned he was one of the Carson City Six, they turned on him right quick and there was nothing Ms. Moon could do to help. With Jubal and Blink dead, he was the last of the fugitives, and the massacre of the posse had fallen on his shoulders.

He sat in a wagon, his hands clasped and bound together in his lap. He tested the rope, but it didn't give. There was no point struggling. There was no point period.

"What day is it?" he asked.

"It's the first of October."

"Today's my birthday."

"I'll be sure to tell the undertaker."

They came to the hanging tree and halted. The bark had been rubbed off a low-hanging bough that was bent like an elbow, and the whitened wood stuck out like a bony arm. A strong breeze blew through the limbs and rustled the leaves. In the distance, the tree line was a gusty blur. Michael had spent the better part of two weeks outdoors, and in all that time he'd never seen trees as beautiful as these. If he could do it all over again, he'd pay closer attention to the music of wind moving through trees.

A white shape emerged from the blur. Michael mistook it for a glimpse of naked trunk exposed by the wind. While the German busied himself with the rope, Michael watched the shape take form: a white horse at full gallop, like an arrow shot from the top of Wotan's Throne. The rider crouched in the saddle, molding his body so perfectly to the beast between his legs Michael couldn't see who was at the reins, but he knew who it was.

The German tossed the rope over the peeling bough and gathered the noose in his calloused hands. Michael stomped his feet to startle the horses, but experience had taught the bounty hunter to anticipate just such a thing, and he socked Michael in the mouth. The blow sent him sprawling into the back of the wagon. The pain was immeasurable but Michael didn't dare shut his eyes. It might all be over when he opened them again. *If* he opened them again.

He spat a bloody tooth at the German, but this was another trick the bounty hunter had seen many times before, and he laughed at the boy's moxie. When the noose was ready, Michael rolled onto his back and kicked at the bounty hunter with his feet, which only served to hasten his capture. The bounty hunter slipped the noose around Michael's neck and cinched it tight. Michael thought he heard the sound of hooves, a rumbling applause, a rapid tumbling over falls. The German heard it, too. He turned in time to catch a tomahawk in the forehead, and the blow made a sound like a melon bursting open. The German let go of the noose and toppled out of the wagon, spooking the horses into a gallop.

"Applesauce," he said.

Michael could see Tonka now, riding high in the saddle, gaining on the wagon. His arms were stippled with leaves and twigs and a dent creased the canister atop his head, splitting his crooked smile in two so that it was half smile, half grimace. Tonka pulled alongside the wagon. He held the reins in his left hand and extended his right to Michael, beckoning him to jump. Michael found his legs, stood at the edge of the wagon, and vaulted into his rescuer's arms. In the space between the wagon and the horse, that split second between this world and the one that comes after, Michael understood what it meant to have a brother.

ACKNOWLEDGMENTS

Thanks to all the good, wise people at Zoetrope Virtual Studios, but especially Melissa Bell, Eric Bosse, Jason DeBoer, Pia Ehrhardt, Mary Kelly, Roy Kesey, John Leary, Shauna McKenna, Justine Wilson, Mary Powers, and Danna Sides. Thanks to Susan Cole at Writers@Work and Cedering Fox at WordTheatre for their support and to the Cline Library at Northern Arizona University for research assistance. Thanks to hangover specialists Tom Ferran and Nathan Cathcart for introducing me to Belfast and the Eastern Sierras, respectively. Special thanks to Tim Poland for lighting the fire.

Jim Ruland is a veteran of the Navy, a part-time English teacher and a creative supervisor at a Los Angeles advertising agency. He is the recipient of numerous awards, including a fellowship from the National Endowment for the Arts. He is a regular contributor to *Razorcake Fanzine*, *The Believer*, and National Public Radio's "Day to Day," and the host of Vermin on the Mount, an irregular reading series in the heart of Chinatown. This is his first book.

ALSO AVAILABLE FROM GORSKY PRESS

DRINKS FOR THE LITTLE GUY by Sean Carswell   paperback — 279 pgs.
"The best book about a carpenter since the Bible."
   —Flipside Magazine

GLUE AND INK REBELLION by Sean Carswell   paperback — 130 pgs.
*"An almost flawless collection of pure literary entertainment on the most down-to-earth,
   real level you could ever hope to find."*
   —*Jay Unidos,* Maximum Rocknroll

THE UNDERCARDS by James Jay   paperback — 100 pgs.
"This book puts the smack-down on poetry!"
   —*Jim Simmerman, author of* Kingdom Come

PUNCH AND PIE edited by Felizon Vidad and Todd Taylor   paperback — 160 pgs.
*"These stories are great. The corporate publishing overlords could never put out an
   anthology such as this."*
   —The Iconoclast

BORN TO ROCK by Todd Taylor   paperback — 318 pgs.
*"When Todd Taylor graces our pages, we believe in punk rock again. And punk rock
gives us hope."*
   —*Ryan Henry,* Thrasher

THE SNAKE PIT BOOK by Ben Snakepit   paperback — 304 pgs.
*"Ben Snakepit captures some moments and moods of our lives so well, like a great song,
   and when it came down to it, I couldn't resist singing along."*
   —*Aaron Cometbus*

WHISKEY & ROBOTS by Bucky Sinister   paperback — 80 pgs.
"I don't really do blurbs anymore, but I really dug this book."
   —*Jimmy Santiago Baca, author of* A Place to Stand

GURU CIGARETTES by Patricia Geary   paperback — 256 pgs.
"Patricia Geary is one of the best fantasy writers working."
   —*Tim Powers, author of* Last Call

BARNEY'S CREW by Sean Carswell   paperback — 237 pgs.
"Sean Carswell is a wonderful storyteller.."
   —*Howard Zinn, author of* A People's History of the United States

FOR A COMPLETE CATALOG OR TO ORDER ONLINE, VISIT:
www.gorskypress.com